D0747075

LINT

STEVE AYLETT'S OTHER BOOKS ARE

Slaughtermatic, Atom, Toxicology, The Crime Studio, Shamanspace,
Only an Alligator, The Velocity Gospel, Dummyland, Karloff's Circus,
Bigot Hall, The Inflatable Volunteer and the *Tao Te Jinx.*

LINT

STEVE AYLETT

THUNDER'S MOUTH PRESS : NEW YORK

LINT

Published by
Thunder's Mouth Press
An Imprint of Avalon Publishing Group Inc.
245 West 17th St., 11th Floor
New York, NY 10011

AVALON

Copyright © 2005 by Steve Aylett

All rights reserved. No part of this publication may be reproduced or transmitted in
any form or by any means, electronic or mechanical, including photocopy, recording,
or any information storage and retrieval system now known or to be invented, without
permission in writing from the publisher, except by a reviewer who wishes to quote
brief passages in connection with a review written for inclusion in a magazine,
newspaper, or broadcast.

Library of Congress Cataloging-in-Publication Data is available.

ISBN 1-56025-684-2

9 8 7 6 5 4 3 2 1

Book design by Sara E. Stemen
Printed in Canada
Distributed by Publishers Group West

for Alan Moore

When the abyss gazes into you, bill it

—Jeff Lint

CONTENTS

ONE

THE BURST SOFA OF PULP

Pulp science fiction author Jeff Lint has loomed large as an influence on my own work since I found a scarred copy of *I Blame Ferns* in a Charing Cross basement, an apparently baffled chef staring from the cover. After that I hunted down all the Lint stuff I could find and became a connoisseur of the subtly varying blank stares of booksellers throughout the world.

Born in Chicago in 1928, Jeff (or Jack) Lint submitted his first story to the pulps during a childhood spent in Santa Fe. His first published effort appeared in a wartime edition of *Amazing Stories* because he submitted it under the name Isaac Asimov. "And Your Point Is?" tells the story of an unpopularly calm tramp who is pelted every day with rocks, from which he slowly builds a fine house. The story already reflected the notion of "effortless incitement" that Lint would practice as an adult. "Jack was fantastic," says friend Tony Fleece. "Went around blessing people—knew it was the most annoying thing he could do. A dozen times, strangers just beat the hell out of him." Lint perfected the technique when he stumbled upon the notion of telling people he would pray for them.

Lint's first novel was published by Dean Rodence's Never Never company in New York. The relationship between Rodence and Lint was one of complete mistrust, rage and bloody violence. When submitting work in person, Lint insisted on appearing dressed as some kind of majorette. "He was a large man and clearly wasn't happy at having to do this," explains Fleece. "He blamed Rodence, was resentful. I still don't know where he got the idea he had to dress that way when handing his stuff in."

The first novel with Never Never was *One Less Person Lying*, in which Billy Stem must tell the truth or be transformed into the average man. Rodence persuaded Lint to change the title word *Person* to *Bastard*. On a night of prepress jitters, Rodence then partially rewrote the final sections of the book so that Stem puts on a space suit and goes berserk, killing an innocent stranger with a large rock. The book was published as simply *One Less Bastard*. In the several years of their association Lint never forgave Rodence for the incident, and often alluded to it by repeated use of the word *bastard* when speaking to him.

Around the time of his second published novel, *Jelly Result*, Lint met his first wife, Madeline, who was attracted to him by a knife scar that led from below his left eye to his mouth. This was in fact a sleep crease and Lint managed to maintain the mistake by napping through most of the marriage. But after five months a bout of insomnia put paid to the relationship and left Lint with nothing to occupy his time but his writing—luckily for the world of literature, as he produced some of his best work at this time, including *Nose Furnace* and *I Eat Fog*, which both appeared on Rodence's new Furtive Labors imprint, and *Slogan Love* with Ace. *Turn Me Into a Parrot* took issue with the fundamentalist notion that the world was only a few thousand years old and that dinosaur bones had been planted by God to test man's faith. Lint asserted that the world was only fifty years old and that the mischievous god had buried sewers, unexploded bombs and billions of people. In my own book *Shamanspace* I make it clear that humanity arrived eons ago but, like a man standing in front of an open fridge, has forgotten why.

By the sixties Lint's reputation was established firmly enough for several feuds to develop with other equally unknown authors, the main one being Cameo Herzog, creator of the *Empty Trumpet* books, who once conspired with Rodence to kill Lint with a truck. (The story is unclear, but it seems that after an unsuccessful try at Lint, they killed or injured the wrong man and had to make reparation to the mob.) The levels to which this feud imploded were difficult for outsiders to understand. Lint and Herzog were once seen glaring silently at each other for seven hours in a freezing lot, each holding a differently colored swatch of velvet.

In 1966 Lint published a series of essays under the ominous collective title *Prepare to Learn*. This included "Running Bent Double—The Poor Man's Protest," "Debate This, You Mother," and "My Beauty Will Blind You," in which he stated: "Some animals have a life span of only a few days. I suspect they eat food only through habit. Why has nature never bred a creature that eats nothing for its few days of life? Such hordes would have a distinct advantage over other species." He then suggests that humanity was meant to be such a species but wrecked everything by stuffing its face the moment it entered the world.

Several of Lint's early books were also being republished by Doubleday and New English Library, and the startled Lint rushed to exploit his raised profile, pulling on a skirt and bursting into the offices of Random House with a proposal he dreamed up on the spot. *Banish m'Colleagues* would tell the story of a bull elephant on its way to the elephant's graveyard, only to find it full of ambulances. The ivory-white confusion of the landscape is a classic Lint image, as is that of Lint being ejected from Random House by twelve security guards. In 1973 Lint instead batted out the trash novel *Sadly Disappointed* about a child who is not possessed by the devil. Published under his Asimov pen name, it is a minor work redeemed only by the parents' laughable attempts at activism. These seem mainly to involve the placing of ignorable gonks on people's driveways—the baffled press is then alerted when the toy is backed over by a car. Lint was at a low, beaten down by a stint in Hollywood that saw his screenplays repeatedly diluted by studio hacks. He felt justly proud of his scripts for *Kiss Me, Mr. Patton* (eventually filmed as *Patton*) and *Despair and the Human Condition* (eventually filmed as *Funny Girl*).

The mid-seventies also saw Lint's incredible foray into the world of action comics with his creation of *The Caterer*. This unfathomable title lasted nine issues, during which the hero was never seen to cook or prepare food in any way. The Caterer's wordless shooting spree in Disneyland in the final issue was as ill-judged as it was relentless, and its blithe use of certain copyrighted characters sank the publishers in legal defense costs.

Lint was by now a Hemingwayesque figure and had developed the ability to speak out of a different part of his beard each time. "Keep 'em guessing," he rumbled. A few observers began to shakily attribute to him some occult transactionary power and a Mrs. Paterson–like ability to project mental images into visual form, if only briefly.

After a second marriage, the Felix Arkwitch trilogy, and short stints in London, Paris and Mexico, Lint returned to the New Mexico of his childhood and produced the first book of his *Easy Prophecy* series, *Die Miami*, which many say was a decoy for more interesting work as yet unearthed. He lived there until his death in 1994, since when Lint scholars have hunted for the gold-dust of lost stories, endlessly analysing the last novel *Clowns and Locusts*, his thankfully incomplete attempt at autobiography, *The Man Who Gave Birth to His Arse*, and his whispered final words, which seem to have been "There's no marrying a cat."

Jeff Lint is buried in a Taos graveyard, his headstone bearing the epitaph: "Don't think of it as a problem, but as a challenge which has defeated you."

This book follows Lint from cradle to grave like an undying mother. I examine his major works in depth, plus many of those that are more obscure, discuss his little-known scrapes with the worlds of movies and comics, and describe my own meeting with the man in 1992. It is a story of disregard, failure, strangely vacant staring and vindication. And it ends in florid dissension as only a truly creative endeavor can.

TWO

WEIRD TALES

Opening joke ∘ *Santa Fe* ∘ *hit by a planet* ∘ *Astounding* ∘ *Mars attacks* ∘
Wall Swordfish Still Alive ∘ *light on the surface* ∘ *crappy story*

"From the instant he was born," said his mother, "that moron was unprofitable."

Lint supposedly rocketed from the womb just as the attending doctor turned aside to share a joke with a nurse. "It was something about penguins," Carol Lint later remarked. "I wasn't too upset when Jeffrey flew out and broke the silly man's jaw. And much too exhausted to laugh, of course." Jeff Lint himself claimed to recall the incident, though he remembered the doctor as a huge white bear and the joke as "an absolute load of garbage." It was July 6, 1928.

Lint's father, Howard, was a middle-of-the-range stockbroker whose motto "All men are created legal" seems to have been designed to be equally useless to all. Lint's only memory of him was a brandy-colored lampshade, a cigar case like a chrome sandwich, and a man whose face had grown to no coherent plan. Jeff and his mother were about to move from Chicago to join Howard in New York when peer pressure and the Wall Street Crash propelled Howard through a twelfth-floor window. Howard Lint became a major player in one of the all-time great suicide dives when another man leapt from the eighth floor directly below him, and beneath the pair a third man rocketed from the fifth. The three dealers stacked up screaming in midair and when this despair sandwich hit the sidewalk on Puce Friday, Lint's childhood was set. He and his mother moved in with her parents in Santa Fe, New Mexico. She kept the Lint name.

Grandpa Ashe was an admirer of George Washington who made a yearly pilgrimage to the Mount Vernon site of the great man's whiskey still. The Ashes were described as "good traitor stock." Lint recalls his grandpa saying, "If we didn't have marked men, people would rise or fall by mere ability." Grandma Ashe carved dolls from pegs and allowed them to crowd the Devant Street house. She said that "carved dolls stick to the rules." There was also a dog with no spark of life in him at all.

Childhood was meant to be gold dust that collects on the windowsill; summer electrons caught in a jar. "But how did I feel when I was a child?" Lint later wrote. "Like I'd been hit by a planet." Lint would dig for hours trying to find a new color, but Carol could always name the colors he found. Jeff became frustrated that there were no gaps between the labels—apparently everything had been filled in before he arrived. "All the fates are spoken for," he thought. "What new thing shall I do with *my* time?"

Sent to the College of St. Seere, Lint kept seeing gaps in answers. He decided early that exasperation professors weren't worth the trouble. They were a bunch of feeble frauds who couldn't keep their abstracts from flapping in the wind. "I was never class clown in school," said Lint in 1971. "But I did have one of those 'downward mouths.'" He escaped through a window, ran across a yard, and collided with a standpipe. "I also burned my leg on an iron bar. I was very spry back then."

In his autobiography Lint scoffed at what is formally registered as the simplicity and innocence of childhood. He believed that the relentless horror of youth, when looked back upon from the fiercer and terminal hell of adulthood, merely seems carefree and simple. "In fact, my dignity went under the lawn mower and that was the last I saw of that."

Lint's mother decided she should educate him at home and Lint began to read voraciously. He was fascinated by Pierre Menard's *Looting of Heaven* and its notion of a "sea-deep book of stirring life." Most men pursue a profession because they stumble upon it so clumsily it runs away. In Lint's case he was scared shitless in 1937 by an issue of *Weird Tales* that had come with them from Chicago as packing material. The story was about furniture coming to life—tables waken everywhere, their spider nature swelling, and humanity finds itself surrounded. A year later all is utterly silent, scream faces immobile in the grain of cupboard wood. The cover of that issue showed an oriental magician beckoning some sort of horned kangaroo from a sewage outlet. Jeff also obtained old copies of *Astounding*, *Amazing* and the Vimana-crazy *Air Wonder Stories*, and after he had shared the magazines with his friend Tony Fleece, the craze spread like an infection. The science fiction pulps concerned themselves with sour-faced gill-men, fossilized Martian railroads and the gee-whiz injuries of alien attack. Jeff enjoyed scaring the timid Amy Beleth with renditions of the stories, which he would elaborate with vague allusions to "the chickens of hell" and "snot bandits." The tomboyish Gabby Janus would not be fazed, however, and told him about a few "gutty goblins" that lived at the bottom of a well. Lint started acting goofy around her and then gave her a poem he had written:

> *I will give you everything*
> *Without regret*
> *Pants and underpants*

Janus has since called him a "tar-eyed romantic."

Amid the frenzy of pulp consumption among the town kids, Lint dreamed one night in 1938 that Martians had landed, red-eyed and in no mood to talk. Then Carol shook him awake and told him that the radio report he had heard through half-sleep was real and that Earth was under attack. Lint did not respond as he should. "He was eagerness incarnate, really," Tony Fleece laughed years later. "We all were. I for one had been boning up on mutants for months and couldn't wait to see an alien, with all that implied in the way of antennae and so forth." But the next day it was revealed as a Halloween prank by Orson Welles. Lint would admire chubby magicians for the rest of his life.

Lint sat down, picked sap from his nose and started a story for *Weird Tales*. "For ages I was fooling around with words that were clearly bewildered at what I was trying to do with them—there was no cooperation at all." Lint wrote "Wall Swordfish Still

Alive" and other creepy concepts like "The Ghosts of a Zillion Slaughtered Cows," but *Weird* didn't bite. In 1940 he sent them "The Glory Key." In this story, gods try to seem mighty though sardined together, packed away by history. They boast at each other like the corpses in Dostoyevsky's "Bobok." "Avoid notice and be free" seems to be the message—one that scandalized this small corner of a nation in which it was already becoming a suspicious act to mind one's own business. "When I showed people the story, several competed with one another in acting shocked, or disapproving, self-effacing, or something like that," Lint explained later, still unsure of motivation. "Being stunned seemed to be the only game in town." Throughout his life Lint experienced phases that he himself barely noticed but that seemed designed to cause anger and regret in those around him. He experimented with addressing people as "my liege" and growling "aye" instead of "yes." During 1970 he addressed everyone as "Petal." In 1983 he began quick-drawing the peace sign like a six-shooter, an act so startling that people would flinch and forget what they were saying. Caul Pin has described Lint's blank expression upon seeing people's reactions to his behavior, and opines that far from being a studied indifference, it was the look of a man so unworldly that he didn't recognize disgrace when it was heaped upon him from a truck. In fact accusatory disapproval was one of the methods listed in "The Glory Key" of avoiding notice—by hiding in plain sight. This was not a method Lint ever practiced. His face was exactly the sort favored by the onrushing fist.

Around the time of these rejections Lint read a story called "The Plank" in *Amazing Stories*—this was about John Derasha, who judged people by how wide they could stare. Those who submitted themselves for his approval were automatically dismissed as insecure wastes of space. The others must be startled into a spontaneous display of eye-stretching. After an entire story following this idiot around as he jumps out at people and gauges their reactions, he gets pounded to the floor by a thug who doesn't like him, and as Derasha lays bleeding in a dark alley we are told he has failed to detect the widest eyes of all—his own during the brutal attack. It was undoubtedly the crappiest story Lint had ever read.

"I knew I could do better than that," he said in his autobiography. "For Christ's sake, an eel could." But Lint's hypothetical eel would be sorely tested in the coming years.

THREE

THE INCREDIBLE FENDER

The Silver Radio ∘ *And Your Point Is?* ∘ *Rouch and Herzog* ∘
food for the moon ∘ *bending words the wrong way*

On October 7, 1940, Navy intelligence analyst Art McCollum wrote an eight-point memo on how to force Japan into war with the United States. Beginning the next day FDR began to put them into effect, but upon the day of the Pearl Harbor attack Lint was still too young to enter the service—in fact he reminisced that his main concern that day was a fascination with the way his reflection stretched along a car fender as though decanting fluidly. "I saw my features being transformed and then shot through what I imagined as a silver Flash Gordon cannon barrel." Lint's story "The Silver Radio" was about such a gun, and a battle in which people fired ideas at one another in an exchange of information,

rather than a war in which informational stance is static and bat-
tles are a parallel, unconnected activity. Lint himself later
described the tale as a "Coblentz imitation" and its most interesting feature today is a chance reference to Bush-Harriman-
Thyssen, which Lint had picked randomly from an old
Herald-Tribune because he had been told by Grandpa Lint that
"names and specifics make for realism." The Emperor Ming–style
villain is called Bank-voor-Handel and craves gold. It is indeed
imitative of the pulpists and seems like a backward step for Lint
since "The Glory Key."

Lint wasn't in love with his chances when he sent it to
Amazing, and the editor Hugo Gernsback wrote back commenting
that the story seemed to have been written in the Berserker tradition. Lint waited a further year before realizing that the letter had
been one of rejection. The next story he sent to *Amazing* was "And
Your Point Is?," the tale of an oblivious pariah, which Lint submitted under the pen name Isaac Asimov. It was published in early
1943 and was a rare occasion of the magazine having a cover created to fit the story rather than the other way around. But after
the fact, Gernsback decided the cover looked like a heap of stink-
ing garbage and resumed the practice of ordering up an octopus, a
spaceman and a screaming woman for the front of every issue.

By the time the story appeared Lint had had several more
stories accepted by *Daring Adventure Stories*, *Troubling Developments* and *Tales to Appall*, which appeared throughout 1943.
Among these were "Digestion and the World," in which the few
remaining humans live in sun-blasted Greenland for half the year
while vampires overrun the rest of the globe, switching places for
the remainder; "The Trunk Show of Everything" in which an

alien plant growing from a large purple bole begins to manifest every possible form on its branches; and "Watch the Endless Shipwreck," in which salt-stained sea zombies converge on a town in search of an affordable tailor. As a result that year Lint received fan mail from a New York pulp fan called Alan Rouch, who turned out to be only a year older than Lint. Also that year Lint first caught the attention of his nemesis Cameo Herzog, a man whose impoverished imagination spawned the statement "Moderation in moderation" and who said of the sky "I've found countless defects in its grain." Herzog regularly described his own heroines as "tasty and pathetic, enticingly vanquished" and his conservative views ("A government is due for removal when dust is deep on its mask") meant that whenever he tried to portray an alien it inevitably showed up in the form of an ostrich in a fez. According to Herzog's review column in the back pages of *Stunning Liberties*, Lint "vexed" him "in a hundred and twenty-seven ways" with his characters' constant mumbling.

Lint was experimenting with what happens when you bend a word the wrong way or when the integuments of the sentence are left visible, a ghost sentence behind the inked one. In time this would allow him to describe political setups many would have thought too lopsided for language. But he was still young enough to envision a life verdant with fees. So he stumbled into the literary world like a bliss-blasted saint, haplessly imaginative and for a good long while unaware of the resentments he was setting to bud.

Lint knew better than to escape while nobody was watching. He asked Rouch to send him a fake letter offering a job in New York. Lint's mother gave him some mittens, and a glare.

FOUR

ANGEL OR SARDINE—LINT AND THE BEATS

Hiding in Columbia ∘ *Campbell* ∘ *Kerouac* ∘ *Benzedrine* ∘ *trying too hard* ∘
appearances ∘ *Gramajo* ∘ *spinal pheasants* ∘ *first shot out of the box* ∘
typography cracked the voices of silence ∘ *Roswell*

Upon arriving in New York, Lint threw his mittens immediately into the trash and went to the halls of Columbia University. It seems that Lint passed a required exam for Rouch and in return stayed anonymously in Rouch's Warren Hall dorm room for several months while Rouch continued to live with his parents. Lint was a happy phantom—he never went to lectures but sucked the library dry and hung out with fellow pulp writer Marshall Hurk, author of "Frontier Bugs and Coffin Lumber" for *Weird*. Lint had set his sights on New York because it was the home of such magazines as *Startling, Astounding, Baffling, Useless* and *Terrible*. He swanned into the office of *Astounding* editor John W. Campbell with a story about a conjuror in a hurry and Campbell laughed in his face, walking ever forward so that Lint had to back away until he was stepping backward onto the sidewalk again. Campbell then stopped laughing and told him to come back when he had something better. Lint returned to the gutter and searched desperately for his mittens, sobbing like an infant. He considered sending the story in again under his Asimov name—Campbell was taking the most appalling trash from the real Asimov at the time— but finally sold it to *Terrible* and was on his way.[1]

Lint was being influenced by his mixing with the nascent Beat scene. Toward the end of 1944 he met Jack Kerouac, who had rented a room at Warren and was devouring books at a similar rate to Lint. On several later occasions he would visit Kerouac's 115th Street apartment, where fellow paleo-cyberpunk William Burroughs was also staying. Seeing the number of Benzedrine inhalers the group were getting through, Lint asked an eminent flu specialist to call at the apartment. When the doctor showed up, the door opened onto a scene combining shock-haired mania with virtuoso lethargy. Lint wrote about the incident in his poem "Middle-distance Hate Decision":

> *smoke hotel*
> *coin eyes*
> *pocket name*
> *and hung answer long gone*

"Perfect grammar eschews screaming," he wrote in a letter to Ernest Hemingway, who was in France observing the 22nd Infantry Regiment's push toward Germany. Hemingway didn't know Lint and knew immediately he didn't want to. Lint continued: "In fact its existence depends on denying that people can make legitimately communicative noise without words."

In February 1945 Lint visited Allen Ginsberg's Hamilton Hall dorm room in the middle of the night and showed him a papier-mâché replica of a New York ambulance with the words MILK ME stenciled upon it. Saying nothing, Lint quickly ran away with the object, leaving Ginsberg—at the time wrestling with the issue of his homosexuality—disturbed by the possible meaning of the incident.

Lint wrote to his mother about "Times Square, a sort of crossroad processing upward of a million idiots a day." But he soon caught Kerouac and Ginsberg's notion of the Square as a big room hanging in space, nothing but smog between it and the universe. Lint told them his vision of the Flatiron Building as "one giant inconvenience." On one occasion Lint fired forty pounds of chili from a turn-of-the-century baseball gun mounted on the roof of a Twenty-third Street apartment block, and eagerly told a baffled Kerouac about it. The young pulpeteer was clearly fumbling his way in the city, but to his credit this seems to be the last recorded instance of Lint trying to impress anyone. From here on he became more real, and a self-amusing trickster. When a shrunken head was hurled into the Angler Bar, it was not confirmed that Lint was responsible.

At seventeen, Lint was shaping up to be a striking figure. "Though he was a big guy," says Hurk, "Lint's face was aquiline and sensitive-looking, with a duckish mouth. I think he looked like a conga eel with a couple of legs."

"He looked like a duck," said Rouch. "And seemed to wear whatever he landed in when he stepped out of bed."

When challenged about his appearance, Lint said, "Appearance runs like clockwork. I always have one." Lint had apparently honed the ability to stand framed in the doorway "like a medieval paintsaint with a halo like a watermelon." Lint had a temperament which was at best parallel to the rest of humanity.

Lint consulted Osman-Spare and struggled with the realities of what could be achieved with the manipulation of symbols. Watching workers in passing night trains, he wondered: Were their flashing silverine flanks those of angels or sardines? Which were crammed upon a pinhead? He tried to accept that we are here to escort the blue photograph of the sky. "All the time eternity plays its angle." He liked Hurk's quip that "every time I look up from my disastrous life I see rubbernecking deities."

These and other issues were thrashed out in the West End Bar, where one of the regulars was Hector Gramajo, a terrible painter more famous for his statement that "Writing is a hostile political act, a way of keeping ideas in a book and out of the way." Cameo Herzog had described him as "a brush with stupidity" but Lint was startled into defending Gramajo when the artist remarked that "Not all colors are in the dictionary." Observing a Gramajo painting that portrayed bats, a man under a glass, and a few dried dates, Lint said the painting was "better than it looks."

"You're not lulling anyone, Lint," said Marshall Hurk. Lint admired Hurk, who once tried to wriggle out of a deadline by claiming to have submitted the manuscript "in the nonvisible spectrum."

Gramajo would later create a pizza carved from redwood.

Lint first met Cameo Herzog in the West End. He complimented Herzog on his story about a giant grasshopper wearing a hat, and Herzog threw a punch. Lint, not yet acquainted with the deceits of the world, watched the onrushing fist with interest. As he later put it, "The sky cohered, birds interlocking." Lint enjoyed the experience, and had nothing to envy in Herzog's work, which read like something pecked out by a dying hen. As Tennessee Williams once said, "Why should I read Herzog? It's easier to leave him helpless." Lint's only written account of the incident seems to have been in a letter to his mother: "Last week I was jeered by a lemon. I consider that an achievement." To Kerouac he said: "I have a private infinity in my pants to take care of." This "trouser-verse" was to feature again in "The Saint of Ozone Park," a Lint story appearing in a 1961 issue of *Floating Bear*.

After the fight Lint had a nightmare about "spinal pheasants," strange bone-helix birds that seemed abjectly real amid a thousand cold complications. In daylight death meshed with life in corners and on the ceiling an insect body's crouch was like a sigilized frown. Lint called Campbell and said he had a story that was "plump as a gorilla's finger" for which he'd accept any offer. Lint was then left with the task of writing the thing, pulling a dress on and going around there. The tale that finally got Lint into *Astounding* was "Ben Carnosaur's Harmless," in which a sauroid businessman's bloody appetites are strenuously ignored by his workmates—a yarn that the cover lines trumpeted with the words "Beautiful woman by day—spindly, boring ant by night!" Herzog's only response to the story was to glare accusingly and wrathfully at Lint when they crossed paths on Third Street, though Lint circled back and met him again, praising his philosophy of being "suspended from a speck" in the hope of receiving another inspiring wound from the dessicated moron.

Lint had been giving Alan Rouch the skinny on pulp writing and Rouch tried his hand, sending *Startling* a story called "The Tripe Chandalier." Retitled "Dragon of the Starry Deeps" and rewritten to include a dragon and exclude any mention of "tripe chandaliers," it appeared two months later, to Rouch and Lint's happy surprise. Rouch was thus set upon the slippery slope to point-blank sobbing and raw yells of bearded despair. "Doubts on either side propel me forward," said Rouch, and Burroughs observed that he "merely looks decisive, an aimless word dropped in ice."

Never Never Publications, which published *Awkward and Inconvenient Stories* (later simplified to *Awkward*), had recently begun putting out entire novels. Lint had sold a story ("Galactic Exasperator") to the magazine and thought the book venture might be ideal for a longer work he was getting together. The book *One Less Person Lying* begins with a Professor Forneus building an energy device to gauge how long it would take for the world to fall apart if everyone was honest. Hours, minutes, seconds? Forneus starts with a two-second burst and millions of people die of massive heart failure. The experience of being honest merely with themselves is like the ground abyssing suddenly beneath them. Only one man, Billy Stem, manages to cling to both honesty and life beyond the burst. He faces his own abyss—that if he ceases to be honest he will join the false morass of the masses. He winds up going to the moon to escape humanity, but another astronaut shows up. This was all to the good for Lint, as the pulps thrived on stories of limited spacemen slugging it out on a barren planet.

"Words are hatless, a geyser," he told editor Dean Rodence, who pretended not to hear him. Rodence agreed to putting out

One Less as a Never Never book, due for fall 1946, as part of a three-book deal.[2] Lint thought his luck had changed—first shot out of the box, his book had been taken on. In celebration he set fire to a rooftop golf range.

As publication approached, Rodence requested changes. He deleted the Huskanoy, a weird brand of photograph with a whiskery root behind it. He struck out "runaway decipherment" and the description of modern culture as "the triumph of complicity." Some readers have compared Lint's books to one of those hazardous gourmet fish with only one nonfatal component. Rodence seemed intent on removing all but the most bland ingredients from *One Less*. He didn't like the sentence "When he spoke, energy would fry his chin" in regard to Professor Forneus. All mention of the Cabaret of Apology were removed, as was Billy Stem's exposing of his "Whitman compass" in the town square. "Is an abdomen's arousal still controversial?" Lint asked wearily. But he made the mistake of conceding to Rodence in changing the title to *One Less Bastard Lying*. "Bastards are always in fashion," Rodence claimed.

When the book finally appeared, Rodence had left off the word *Lying* from the title and the ending had been mysteriously rewritten to feature a maniacal killing frenzy, with Billy Stem hurling a boulder onto his fellow man. Lint burst into Rodence's office with his arms already raised in a strangling pattern, connecting with Rodence's throat and twisting it like an industrial sink pipe. Marshall Hurk was no more impressed than Lint. "The first question I asked Lint about that book was how fast he was driving when he hit it." Campbell did not even dimly suspect that it was any good. Herzog wrote: "Instinct should look where it's going." And veteran pulpist E. E. Smith said of Lint: "Yes, I read one of his books: *One Less Bastard*, if the title on the cover were to be believed. When I finished the volume, I wept with relief."

When Lint read about the Roswell incident in 1947 he was taken back to the canceled Mars Invasion of 1938—the present incursion, too, was quickly written off. Maybe the Martians really have only half an arse, he reflected.

FIVE

"MONSTROUS POET ALARMS SHOPPERS"

The joker ∘ *covers and headlines* ∘ *escape artist* ∘ *The Day Maggots Sing* ∘
smashing the world ∘ *this bad reputation* ∘ *Rosebud Investment*

"Distract one ear, scare the other, steal everything," said Edward
Bernays of the strategies of government. Lint was adept at the
first two stages of this game plan but neglected the third, and it
is left to us to conclude what his goal was in screwing a snail into
a light socket. Though Lint claimed that "Nothing unites vampires like a sleeping vicar," it won him few friends and had him
penciled in as an enemy for at least eight of his acquaintances.

Lint would allude to this time in his story "Ghostly Hens
Forever, Forever," published as "The Man with the Stupid Arm" in
issue 87 of *Terrible Stories*. In those days the tales in such magazines were often commissioned to conform to cover artwork

already created, and in this case editor Hugh "Banzer" Dewhurst
wanted Lint to write around a splash depicting a gardener being
savaged by a sort of space-lobster. In "Ghostly Hens," which was
already written, Lint had talked about his days in late-forties New
York through a metaphor. A hale fellow sits contentedly on a rural
porch; he reaches for his pipe and finds that a sort of ectoplasmic
hen is bulging from his arm. He laughs, then screams, then
becomes complacent, and then loves the creature—and then
cycles through all these emotions repeatedly as time passes
around him. "He looked at a kind of dark finality through wind-
blown stirring nausea and proportion surrounding his sidewalk.
He was as unconcerned and killable as a flower, from whose death
as little can be gained as that of a flower. A lifetime passed in a
minute." When suddenly his wife pops out of the house with a
sandwich, the break from eternity ejects him from the porch and
sends him wheeling through the neighborhood, flinching as
though dodging shrapnel. "And it wasn't even fun," the tale concludes. For *Terrible Stories*, Lint changed the hen to a space-
lobster and wrote in a covering note to Dewhurst: "Got yourself
into quite a pickle haven't you?" Lint's relationship with Dewhurst finally reached an end with Lint's 1960 story "Feelgood," in
which the hero awakes *Day of the Triffids*–style to find the world
empty of people and wanders blissfully free of harassment for the
rest of his life. The character's transition from cautious optimism
to boundless joy is superbly handled, though Dewhurst removed
several scenes where the protagonist spontaneously climaxes
while walking down the deserted streets.

In 1949 Lint managed to convince the hapless Alan Rouch
that he could win the Nobel Prize by disguising his head as a giant

eyeball. The smartly dressed Rouch looked striking with the huge orbit atop his shoulders and attracted a crowd of gawkers in the New York Public Library, explaining the grand aim of his act when a journalist arrived. This encounter resulted in the headline STARING IDIOT PUNCHES REPORTER and, feeling bad over the stunt, Lint announced to the same reporter that he himself intended to marry a hen. Presented with the paper by a beaming Lint, Rouch pointed out to him that the headline ECCENTRIC AUTHOR MARRIES HEN topped a story about how "author Alan Rouch openly admits to his lust for poultry." Lint was dogged by lazy journalism throughout his life and among his bannered outings are PULP WRITER'S PUMP-ACTION HEAD CLAIM (*San Francisco Chronicle*), SF AUTHOR IN "CHARMED WONDERBOY" OUTBURST (*Los Angeles Times*) and WRITER IS MADE OF CHIMP MEAT (*Maine Catholic Record*), though each of these seems to have some obscure origin in truth.[3]

During his erstwhile Beat phase Lint was an enthusiast of close-up magic despite his never really mastering the crucial "magical" phase of a single trick, a shortcoming he tackled by punching the observer's lights out just before the moment of wonder. Thus any onlooker who chose the fist containing the palmed coin would instantly feel that fist slamming into his nose. When later challenged by the victim, Lint would feign bafflement and claim that the trick had been completed successfully, without violence and to the victim's awe and delight. In San Francisco in 1955 Lint was cornered by Ginsberg and Kenneth Rexroth into doing a trick before an audience at the Six Gallery and felt it necessary to go berserk, spraying the cards at the volunteer's face and firing a starting pistol into the panicking crowd.

More apposite to his real vocation was Lint's regular appearances in public in a fright wig and sharpened wooden teeth.
Taking up a place on some busy thoroughfare, he would throw his
arms wide and volley his verse at nobody in particular. MON-
STROUS POET ALARMS SHOPPERS, announced a headline in the
Washington Post of March 18, 1954: "Customers of Woolworth's
department store on Monday were frightened by a freakish man
with unkempt hair and sharp teeth, who delivered a stream of
rhyming gibberish. His theatrics attracted the attention of store
police, who claim that he 'disappeared' before they could detain
him." Lint's favorite recitations included "I Can See You Eddie,"
"Gripe into This Horn," and a poem about his cogitations on
whether to join the army, "The Day Maggots Sing":

The day maggots sing
I will join the army
I will join the army
The day maggots sing
When they do, call me
Maybe they swing
I will join the army
The day maggots sing

Later appearances of the "monstrous poet" were reported to
involve the violent death of several onlookers, but these are
thought to have been the work of an opportunist copycat.

The golden age of Lint's pranks happened to coincide with
the rise of the McCarthyist commie scares and as early as 1949 he
had infiltrated a crowd picketing the Waldorf in protest against

Shostakovich—among those with banners yelling GO BACK TO
RUSSIA WITH YOUR COMMIE PROPAGANDA, Lint paced about with a
sign that stated I'M GROWING FINS. Lint was twitted the same year
when three friends dressed as cops raided his apartment and
found him forcing a bust of Lenin down the toilet.

One of Lint's many false starts to a mainstream media career
occurred as a result of the blacklisting of suspected communist
sympathizers in showbiz. Up-and-coming CBS exec Douglas
Norton came to Lint in 1951 and told him he could make good
money filling in for the commie scriptwriter Ordal Lissitsky. Lint
took him at his word and banged out scripts in which shiny-faced
families talked about how things were "better in the Soviet
Union" and Irish cops chided, "From each according to his ability,
to each according to his need," all delivered in the blandly mirth-
ful style of the cookie-cutter sitcom. Norton burst into the script
room and shook Lint by the shoulders, shouting that he'd
"smashed the world" with his craziness, then mistook Lint's blank
incomprehension for poker-faced cool. Norton grabbed Lint and
tripped over the carpet, pulling him to the floor and laughing
despite himself. Lint stood up with dignity, brushed himself down
and left the room in silence. He would have nothing more to do
with television until the disastrous *Catty and the Major* more than
a decade later.

In April 1952 Lint appeared before the House Committee on
un-American Activities pretending to be Elia Kazan, following it
up with a parodic advertisement in the *New York Times*. "Kazan
himself didn't mind," Lint later claimed, "as it got him out of having to appear or be blamed for anything that was said." Among the
things Lint said in his stead were, "What's wrong with looking at

the cupboard?" and "Clifford Odets has tomatoes for eyes," then repeating, "Eyes." Lint felt it important to emulate Kazan quite closely, up to and including his being a spineless mass. The *Times* advert called communism an "alien conspiracy" and claimed that "liberals must speak out." It was, at the time, Lint's best and most sustained absurdist work. This was still seven years before the revelation that Senator McCarthy lay every morning in a bathtub brimming with liquidized doves.

To his credit, Lint allowed none of these antics to slow his progress in the expanding pulp market. As the pulps entered the fifties and recovered from the wartime paper shortage, dozens of new magazines appeared, with titles like *Thrilling Wonder Stories, Beyond Absurdity, Swell Punch-Ups, Damaging Claims* and *Pull the Other One.* The covers invariably depicted bug-eyed humans examining receipts or fifties housewives closing the window on bewildered aliens. Between 1950 and 1955, Lint sold 123 stories to *Astounding, Bewildering, Confusing, Baffling, Frazzling, Scalding, Mental, Marginal, Fatal, Useless, Appalling, Made-Up* and *Meandering,* as well as the short-lived *Completely Unbelievable Explanation, Maggoty Stories, Way Beyond Your Puny Mind, Overelaborate Alibis* and *Maximum Tentacles.* The latter over-lapped into what today would be called the "specialty" market, promising "a tentacle in every sentence," and Lint had trouble modifying his story "The True Origin of the Magi" to fill this pre-scription. There were several such dubious titles, *Denim Bear, Train Epiphany* and *Commercial Rose Cultivation* foremost among them. Strapped for cash, Lint tried to write a story appealing to all three of these titles—this resulted in the groundbreaking "Rosebud Investment," a tale of exuberance and paranoia. The tale begins with Ben Marax sitting on a train—he suddenly realizes that he's been living in a fool's paradise. These things he calls "bantamweight roses" are in fact grenades, but their explosion sequence is so subtle and obscure that human beings fail to notice the event. Aliens voided the objects into our dimension without understanding our value system—humanity never even noticed or valued the portion of themselves destroyed by these colorful antenna land mines. "And that part is," says the appalled alien leader, a denim bear, "the SOUL!"

Lint eventually sold the tale to *Maggoty Stories*.

Ironically it was this tailor-made yarn that led Lint to shout defensively at Cameo Herzog: "Your body picks up a pen and it aligns to others. Mine flies all over the place."

Lint's prolific output provoked Gernsback to accuse him of writing with a rake dipped in ink.

But how did Lint write so many stories and what was the nature of the pulp world in which he worked?

SIX

"I CAN TAKE ANYTHING": THE PULP LIFE

High pulp ∘ *Perry Street* ∘ Baffling Belly Stories ∘ *a crystalline associate* ∘
Alvarez ∘ *toasting the Bread of Shame* ∘ *release the tigers*

Despite his hell-for-leather delineation of an existence withered by compromise, Lint never wanted for female company. Women were curious about this fellow who, according to Kerouac, "walked around like some angelic oaf" and talked about the tilted cities of Mars in a tone of bored resignation. Lint responded to flirtation by yelling "Attract *me* will you?" with all the panoramic heroism of resistance. The woman who could tackle or overlook this was a catch indeed and Lint took up with such a catch in 1953, renting a sort of imploded loft on Perry Street with Emily Abodon, a dressmaker. Lint began churning out stories while Abodon ran off creations in which he could deliver the typescripts. They were scallywags on the up.

The pulps devoured galactic stories without strict regard for payment and the typical editor was a broken man yet to realize he was in need of repair. A case in point was Hugh "Banzer" Dewhurst of *Terrible Stories*, who frantically admitted his aim was to "just fill the damn thing" with "jelly, charge-beams, idiots—who am I?" and smacked at his own head until his hair was wild and conditionless. Despite this the pulps were a welcome gash of fluorescence in a culture that Lint described in "The New Testament of Cigarettes" as "a dowager dealing manners out of a purse." But Lint tried to inject an element of health-giving betrayal into the sort of gassy hokum that was proving popular with pulp audiences at the time. Hooked initially by Lint's ludicrously bad dialogue such as "It's a sort of sensory potbelly, bouncing toward us" and his tendency to describe characters as entering rooms with "gills blazing," readers would stay to find out whether the pig mentioned in the opening paragraph would reappear as a significant part of the story.

Following the success of "Rosebud Investment" and its declamatory punch ending, Lint repeated the formula in a string of stories which pulp historian Mike McCurry describes as "garbage": "He kept doing these stupid endings where the main character or villain turns round and announces some revelation, but it got pretty predictable pretty fast." Such as the story "I Married a Trash Compactor" in which, after marrying a trash compactor and suffering the many adversities pursuant to that mistake, the hero turns to us, the readers, and states, "It was bound to happen, because...*I married a trash compactor!*" The element of surprise was a distant memory when Lint submitted a tale in which a postman wakes up early, goes on his rounds, drinks some coffee, finishes his work, leaves the office, then stops to announce, startled by doom, that he did it all because he is a postman. Lint was by this time eating nothing but kelp and some kind of papery gauze, according to Abodon. The loft was a dented hell of beaten hay and the margins that Lint cut off because they "twisted his melon."

Lint's own interpretation of those days is more hallucinatory—in a 1971 interview he said of his Village years: "The apartment gradually became a hangout for the living dead." And later he claimed again: "The befuddled undead kept splintering the doors and shambling around like simplicity itself till someone had the smarts to behead them. That's the style of interruption I had to contend with."

Abodon encouraged him to spend more time with his buddies at Fugazzi's but Lint would enter the bar wearing a papier-mâché Alsatian head—and this almost thirty years before Reagan's inauguration. Marshall Hurk recalls: "He'd stand there tensing his stomach and say, 'Punch me—I can take anything.' Of course because of the false head we didn't know which of us he was talking to, so we all hit him at the same time. It was brutal."

"He's a dangerous bastard," said Herzog at the time. "The next thing will be the police."

But the next thing was "Chest-deep in My Own Belly," the first of Lint's alarming "belly stories," which he claimed—to any editor who would listen—were popular on the streets. Paul Steinhauser of *Baffling Stories*, a shell of a man at best, was out-of-touch enough to believe him and published them as fast as Lint could churn them out, including "The Belly Cannot Lie," "Woe Unto My Belly," "Belly Invasion," "My Belly Is an Eye," "My Eye

Is a Belly," and "Look Out—Bellies." Steinhauser found himself with such a backlog of belly stories that he attempted to get rid of them in a special belly issue, *Baffling Belly Stories*—only to find more belly stories coming in every day and mere incomprehension on the streets. Many of the new belly stories were from other authors, who had taken note of the editor's apparent thirst for them. Rouch wrote three in one day—"Escape from the Belly," "My Belly Will Be Sainted Today," and "Liberation Belly—an Odyssey into the Belly of the Belly." Steinhauser was bewildered by the onslaught and the fact that he had become known as the Belly Guy. Writers stopped sending him normal SF, drawling in bars that "no—he only takes belly stories these days," and beginners were "forcing bellies" into their tales long after Lint had moved on. *Baffling Stories* sank under the weight of this manufactured craze, and Lint would not encounter Steinhauser again until the editor's surprise attack on him in 1973.

Lint's new pastures after the belly series were gated by his meeting with the literary agent Robert Baines. Lint was unusual among pulp story writers in that he had already had a novel published and Baines claimed he could help Lint to smash upward in the literary world. He was instrumental in getting *Jelly Result* sold to Doubleday, and then slipped into the dormant insectile state common to agents while siphoning 15 percent of all Lint's subsequent earnings. The contract he left in testament was labyrinthine. Lint was later to parody agent catatonia in his story "The Crystalline Associate" but this was as nothing compared to the real story: one of souping flesh and unbreathable air.

However, in 1954 this was all to come and the sale of *Jelly Result* had Lint in a froth of optimism as to his prospects. "I'll probably bake a pie for my famous friends every Wednesday," he speculated in his notes, "and push my luck a little further each time." Next to this note is a sketch of Lint with an ax.

Among Lint's present friends was José Alvarez, a highly strung Cuban who had penned a poem called "Magnificent Stallion Humiliation" and felt that this justified his every emotional and financial demand upon society. He never wrote another work but insisted that he was "the greatest of poets and worthy of praise." Alvarez was irrationally terrified of rainfall and Lint delighted in tormenting him by entering the room shaking an umbrella. He also tormented Alvarez by addressing him as "Lenny" and telling everyone he was a "gifted barber." People continually approached the erstwhile poet requesting a haircut and, rebuffed, would cajole him with cries of "Just a trim, Lenny" until he exploded with rage. Lint started the rumor that Alvarez would give a haircut in exchange for an umbrella of any quality. The Cuban was by now phobic about umbrellas and tried to strangle Herbert Huncke, who had staggered up to him with rheumy eyes and a dead cocktail parasol. Lint continued to favor story series and produced four tales about José's antics: "False Hope for Lenny," "Lenny Turns Violent," "Lenny Burns His Bridges and Is Not Bailed Out," and "Lenny Will Never Be More Than a Somewhat Gifted Barber." This stream of rubbish was to gain a terrible significance less than a decade later.

Lint's pulp story career was at its most productive in 1954 and this was down to a writing routine that eliminated anyone who came near him—or attempted to. "I went to see him at the Perry Street loft," says Marshall Hurk, "and as soon as I entered he pushed a hen toward me—a live hen—with the tip of his boot.

Anyone else would be honking with laughter as they did that but he was completely silent. Even the hen was silent. Freaked me out." Terry Southern also commented on Lint's habits at this time: "He had a sort of mantra he repeated, it was 'Great crowd tonight—release the tigers.' But he'd walk toward you saying it louder and louder until your whole body was filled with a kind of core panic and you ran like hell."

It was during these hen-shoving, mantra-bellowing days that Lint labored over the story that would grow to become *Jelly Result*.

SEVEN

JELLY RESULT

Rain upon travelers ∘ *Eterani* ∘ *Valac infects his punishment and*
backs it up into the community ∘ *the coining of Fanny Barberra* ∘
shallow and deep vanishing ∘ *like a cat* ∘ Slogan Love ∘
relief disguised as penance ∘ *circus of glossolalia* ∘ *Maurice Girodias*

Lint was ambushed by his second novel—what started as a fairly standard tale of sagging clock ducts grew out of size, provoking Emily Abodon to issue an ultimatum, "The story, or me." Baffled, Lint was still waiting for a verb when Abodon slammed from the apartment and left him to his work. Lint was experimenting (perhaps in an attempt to profit from the painful experience of *One Less Bastard*) with the replacing of a single word throughout his already published works—the most successful of these was his substituting the word *jelly* for *belly* in his Belly series[4]—he made a thick binder marked JELLY RESULTS, alongside DEATH RESULTS, SNOT RESULTS and EXHAUSTION RESULTS, then began weeping at what his life had become. He fell to the floor like a faulty assistant and saw a vision of bodies located below their impatient souls. "They behave like rain upon travelers," he thought, seeing those spirits. "We are a circus of ourselves. We make the sleeve. We the alteration." The strong moment disappeared. "The zeal here is a captivity," he wrote in his notebook. "Some scallywag has misconnected the reward to cancer."

In the novel *Jelly Result*, half of Eterani city is exactly the same as the other half, because the authorities don't have enough ideas to cover the whole area. Among its citizens only Valac is aware of this. "This furniture happens every day," he complains, and sets out to find how many recurrences exist of each object. Should a slight variation be counted as a different idea? "The happy clock is in several places, magic as yes and no." Both versions of each object can be altered a little, but when Valac tries to introduce something new he is physically attacked by the environment, which tries to digest and redistribute him into the architecture. *Jelly Result* features the first appearance of equalizer pests, fatal gizmos that Lint never really described except to repeatedly deny that they were "made of wax."

Finally, Valac distracts the city by shuffling the two halves together so that the paucity of ideas is not so strikingly apparent (thus Eterani becomes like any human city). The city itself, now forgetfully convinced that it is interesting, loses its defensiveness. When Valac introduces a genuinely new notion (in this case the innards of a mirror packed into a transparent dome covered in converging lampreys hewn from black stone and incorporating a few simplicity junctions for breathing) the authorities are so sure that it should lead to disaster, they order such a disaster by the back door. Emboldened, Valac infects his punishment and backs it up into the community—a titanic elemental wall hits the city, percentages stretch in the boiling air and molten angels blot out of the walls. The book ends with the city mayor expressing ominous dissatisfaction with the polychrome result: "The instant the sky was launched that morning it became obvious that so vivid a reality was unacceptable." The world is not yet won.

Jelly Result had an impact among those clipped to the main nerve. It briefly popularized the use of the term *hand expiry* for death, as well as the phrase "I alone am indecent enough to say it aloud." It also included the trope "Barricades stop the knowing of both sameness and difference, Fanny Barberra," a slogan that was to appear on some of the larger and more expensive protest banners in the sixties. Eterani itself has the feeling of Hinton's flatlands, but is surrounded by Lint's casual dimensional contortions, such as the digression on the difference between "shallow vanishing," by which you walk around a fold in the air and disappear apparently into nowhere, and the art of "deep vanishing," by which you simply walk directly away.

The book did badly with the critics. Its moral demanded a grave so sophisticated it would have been easier to keep it alive, but Lint's speculations upon "a society different enough to have a different corpse decay rate" had overstepped the mark. The mainstream ignored him like a cat. Meanwhile Cameo Herzog, now a reviewer for the *New York Times*, told everyone Lint was "as vague as an embalmer's answer." Lint thought it was the only funny thing Herzog ever said and repeated it to everyone, once dressing up as a turtle to enhance the impersonation. This was to step up a one-sided feud that would span years and create publicity for both without any real effort on Lint's part.

Making notes for the book *Slogan Love*, Lint was becoming a master of double-jointed sentences that could go in any direction at any time. The world of *Slogan Love* is one of necessity unmet. "An optimist has nothing but miracles to rely on," he wrote, and portrayed streets clotted with rotting bodies. Into this land walks Isou, declaring a philosophy called Haagenti. "We have limitations to remind us that someone somewhere hates us with a passion," she tells the city council who, about to abscond in a helicopter, are annoyed at her sudden appearance. They are required to listen in poses of exaggerated focus. "Success in a zoo is still failure," she tells them.

"Sometimes even a cat wants to act stupid and stagger about," the mayor complains.

The farcical nature of the book, in which people lock one another in rooms and run around gathering what they might need when they reach a safe outpost, ends with Isou herself reaching the roof and ascending in the helicopter, her blank face seeming to scorn the enraged, impotent bureaucrats below. At the same moment several identical helicopters arise from administrative buildings elsewhere in the city, containing identical women.

Lint toyed with the book for a while as he worked up the incredibly strange *I Blame Ferns*. Dodging creditors, Dean Rodence was changing addresses on a regular basis without telling anyone where he was going. After one of his absences he complained bitterly at *Slogan Love* going out as an Ace Double with Jim Dewar's *Quantum Strumpet*. Lint told him he would give him the next one. He was already working on two—*I Blame Ferns* and *Nose Furnace*.

Ferns follows Jaen Amober from the moment he awakes, eavesdropping on the theories that flare through his brain. "The average person happens to think about lobsters perhaps once a month. *Now* tell me a chef hasn't got something wrong with him!" His obsession with chefs allows some room for thoughts of ships ("Ships like vast zipper fastenings—it won't work"), exile ("Exile is relief disguised as penance"), and pigs ("Pigs are all about expediency"). Though Lint denied it, scholars have suggested that Amober is a schizophrenic attempting to draw meaning from everything that meets his eye—"Eyes are the sphincters of reality," says Vaneigem—thus the pages are rammed with data. "Modern architecture is about endurance on all sides," says Amober as he walks through the city. "Has there ever been a neutral sky?" he asks, looking up. "No one is more beautiful than the romantic partner of an oaf," he observes, seeing a happy couple. "Pasta is a triumph of consensus over self-respect," he says, passing a bistro. "Bandy arms like an orangutan," he sneers, observing an orangutan at the zoo. "Excessive confrontation is a kind of evasion," he thinks, watching a cop.

He returns again and again to the subject of chefs. "All day long the chefs are unaffected by my words," he grieves, crossing the road. Has he after all become a lobster's shell stuffed with human meat, as he had feared in his early years? "Ambiguity is what a dog leaves behind when it gets in the car," he reflects. Catching sight of a fern bush in all its complication, he is torn with horror at its skeletal darkness. "I am your life's fragile sick zigzag," he hears it whisper.

Right at the end of this daylong voyage, Amober enters the rear of a restaurant, pulls on his bib and hat, and starts dicing carrots. The final sentence, *"Here he stood, sorting tasty biology for slobs."*—is one of the most dreamlike and weightless in literature.

Lint had just put on something particularly slutty to take the manuscript around to Rodence, when a parcel arrived containing a slab of bloody meat and a note, in Rodence's hand, saying WARE CAN I BE?

Exasperated with this nonsense (and not realizing that Rodence was directing him in code to his new office in the meat-packing district), Lint sought out a fleet publishing house that didn't mess around or withhold money.[5] Ginsberg put him in touch with the Olympia Press in Paris, run by the unbelievably dodgy Maurice Girodias. Ginsberg assured Girodias that *blame* was American slang for *fuck* (and the book does appear in his 1959 catalogue as *I Fuck Ferns*). Lint never received his advance from Girodias, who later sold *Ferns* to Ace. The Ace edition's cover erroneously stated that Lint had been the author of *Quantum Strumpet*. "It's times like this," Lint told Alan Rouch, "I wish I was indifferent. Or a seal."

EIGHT

SPARKING MAD

Critical reaction ∘ Nose Furnace ∘ *Rouch rumble* ∘ *reverse template* ∘
Cheerful When Blamed ∘ *coast to coast* ∘ *for the birds* ∘
everything is plentiful here

"The narrator appears to be constructing a raft with which to escape our interest," stated Cameo Herzog in his 1958 review of *Nose Furnace*, "and in this the finished structure succeeds admirably." Herzog had finally given up on his unpopular *Shadow*-style superhero, the Bailiff, and was to be seen shuffling down Forty-second Street muttering about the cash value of his forehead. Bitter in lean times and fearful of loss in palmy days, he took to review work like a chimp to a centrifuge. Disregarding the merits of *Jelly Result* was one of his first duties for the *New York Times*, but like so many of Lint's works, *Nose Furnace* was like a red rag to this sad man. He was baffled and enraged by the so-called eel prejudice exchange near the start of the book, to which every character refers back with enigmatic addenda:

"And don't come back until you're prejudiced against eels."

"Eels, eh? In sunshine?"

"Sunshine? Well, wherever you find them."

"In sunshine?"

"All right."

"Chew them up?"

"Eh?"

"Chew them up?"

"Okay, whatever you say—chew them up, chew 'em."

"Chew the eels?"

"Okay."

"I will then—see you later."

"Yeah, take it easy."

"All I need to know is," Herzog emphasized, "does he think we're fools with nothing important to do? The man says, 'I am turning into a draped bundle of kelp—adore me.' Must we do so? *Must we help this drawling layabout to pay off his gambling debts while he purportedly becomes a sea weed?"*

Lint marveled at the rage he could incite without effort. When Rouch tried to bring him and Herzog to amiability in the West End, Herzog referred to Lint as a "lugubrious obstacle." Lint responded characteristically, as he recalled later: "Rather than be doomed and exhausted by my own explanations, I carved the shape of a bell into the chair." Herzog would thenceforth describe Lint as "sparking mad" and, sustained by a war chest of unimaginative sarcasm, attack him at every opportunity.

As the cream horn of the high pulp crowd, Lint made himself a hostage to fortune by talking back to books, breaking into antique stores to carve spooky puppets from the priceless wares, wearing a stupid fur-lined jacket, and saying "Here come my unhappy countrymen" whenever friends approached. Rouch urged him to simmer down, for the sake of the pulp community. This from a man who once pitched a novel with the words "Discreet knock at door, enter to discover the hero in diapers. Bingo."

Lint often inveigled Rouch into his schemes. Ducking down an alley, they would dress up as ants and beat the hell out of anyone who approached. Lint later described it as a guerrilla tactic to reinstitute the lost significance of psychogeographical space. One such alley gave Lint an unusual insight, a superdeep template that reversed past the zero inch marker into negative. The neon vision ended up in a story called "The Undismantled Fella." Following the theory that everything in the world was made of information, the hero looks into walls but is surprised to find that the information therein has nothing to do with being a wall ("the atomic stuff therein didn't know it was a wall"). Some is about infinitely slow friction, much is impossible to categorize and the rest is incomprehensible. He winds up in cranky corners, assailed by frazzling dimensional site-lines that carve past his eyes with the smell of scorched air.

Before *Nose Furnace* appeared in the States, a Lint story collection, *Cheerful When Blamed*, had appeared with Rich and Cowan in Britain. They would take a second collection, *Mask of Disapproval*, around the time Lint parted company with *Terrible* in 1960. But a few copies of *Cheerful* made their way unheralded to the States and Herzog felt all the more bitter and threatened by Lint's apparently easy and prolific output. Lint himself had forgotten about *Cheerful* and later claimed never to have seen the article condemning it in the *Boston Globe*.

Cheerful When Blamed contained a pretty good selection of Lint's fifties-era stories, many having first appeared in *Baffling, Terrible, Stupid* and *Just Plain Awful* up to 1956. Among them were "Badge of Honor," describing those imprisoned for killing mimes, "Microdestiny," in which everyone must wear "corpuscle identity skirts" or be shot at a checkpoint, "The Tenth Deface-ment," which features rounded crablike creatures that are basi-cally sprung human kneecaps escaping to their independence, and Lint's attempt at an Asimovian short story, "The Robot Who Couldn't Be Bothered." Most of the stories were gimmicky and this helped Herzog consolidate his criticism of Lint in the broad-sheets. But though he may have pushed his luck with "The Rustic Intensity of Benny's Truss," Lint touched a nerve with his take on religion, "I'm Not Listening." Lint would often point out the dis-comfort natural selection provides for the well-intentioned, while providing pleasure for the deadly and the low. "Euphoric corpses allow for no prophet," he mused in his notes. "Birds despise laws that profit by their absence." In the story, God shows up at the expected moment of an eclipse and chirps, "I canceled the plane-tary conjunction—it's too, too tedious."

Cameo Herzog, who held the opinion that "hens fail to speak because the New Testament says so," was incensed at the story and most of his *Globe* article was taken up with an attack on it and its author, a slobbering maniac who had famously "married his

own hair." He commented that Lint's philosophy was "a lacy circuit of which the genius of total enigma can make anything. It is a
mere percolator twist in the common knowledge." This work, he
said, was the product of a botched mind. "The childishness of such
remarks as this: 'When sin made its way even into Eden, it's no
wonder certain realities had to be acknowledged.'!" Herzog
reserved special ire for the portrayal of a priest who would point at
things with his elbows just to be special. "So cruel to eliminate my
afternoon with this gibberish, when I was quite prepared to take it
seriously. Lint's madness is beyond dispute."

Though Herzog's own works were brazenly recycled bullshit,
Lint never bothered attacking them. The one time Lint attempted
a review piece, it was an account of the new Egyptian display at
the Milwaukee Museum in 1960. "Every single exhibit was epi-
cally pointless," he wrote. "The flat tones of old mummy-britches
made me moan to my lover, 'Kill me darling, so I can die by something lusty rather than fading like Edwardian curtains. I am in
hell!' At that point even the mummy's curse would have struck me
as a blessing. We were loudly discovered behind an old jar, grabbing at each other in an effort to stay awake."

The lover he was grabbing behind the jar was Madeline Botis.
In 1960 Lint woke up in Berkeley and decided to live there—he
could see a palm tree and a funny dog from where he lay. Visiting
the Caper Club, he saw Botis performing "Newspaper Does Not
Absorb Blood" and fell for her immediately, suggesting to her that
they get married in front of God and everyone. He had to be wres-
tled from the stage so that she could finish the agonized recital.

A week later Alan Rouch got a letter from Lint saying he
should come over: "away from Herzog and his graph paper barri-

cades. Everything is plentiful here. Blue skies, bloodshot eyes, and tremendous scope for skylarking. Outrun a carrot, falter, find yourself steadied by it in a sportsmanlike way. Become only briefly ashamed. The lesson is a long-term one. Be brave."

NINE

TURN ME INTO A PARROT

Sigil train ∘ *alien designs* ∘ *quantum punchline* ∘ *craw wafers* ∘
bug hunt ∘ *first lines* ∘ *"we are imperiled"* ∘ *tough*

In Berkeley, Lint tried to blend strict writing discipline with the new demands of married life. His afternoon schedule was interrupted only by his "time of worship," which was in fact the hour during which he knelt with his face buried between Madeline's legs. "As far as I'm concerned her eyelids wrap fruit," he wrote to Marshall Hurk, "(a good thing)."

This routine produced the last big burst of Lint stories before his move into full-time book writing. In "The Pernoctalian," Sam Kallat lays out a model train track that coincidentally forms a demonic invocation symbol when activated. The satanic fiend that appears is scruffy, patriotic and anxious, and appears to be based

on Richard Nixon. It seems to believe its purpose is to pump gaso-
line, and asks Kallat if he needs diesel. In "The Neck Century"
human forces cancer across the galaxy, boring everyone they
meet. The aliens they encounter always find a way to excuse
themselves, claiming a death in the family or "matters at present
beyond your comprehension," and then hide at home until
humanity has moved on. Sci-fi fans at the time complained at the
forms taken by Lint's aliens, as he rarely went for the apple-green-
headed Martian type. In regard to the preoccupied invaders of
"Well-made and Unseen Save by Angels," Lint commented in
Bloody Fantastic Idea: "Imagination wholly determined the creatures that issued from the nebulae, so I thought I'd make them
huge boiled-candy prairie dogs. We first see them in a solemn
glowing department store. They don't give a damn about the
pants. Right off, I liked them." More prairie dogs showed up in
"Whiskers Are Never Colossal." At this time Lint went through a
phase of describing everything as "colossal," mangling perfectly
good stories with this perversion. For instance, "The Colossal
Bastard" (published in *Why?*) is about the moment that God creates humanity. "I'll just fill it with blood and push it out there," he
decides, then returns to telling a long, involved joke to Satan. The
joke is so complicated that it has several interlocking punch lines,
resembling overall a bit of Escher architecture. The first man,
dimly overhearing part of this quantum punch line as he is dis-
carded into the world, spends the rest of his life trying to recon-
struct it, and thus a dozen political and religious systems are set
into motion. "An Ominous Mirth" begins with city officials
expressing indignation at an elated wretch and his "untoward
glow." Imprisoning the man, they find the city transformed into a

cold white rose garden dotted with heavy gold infants. "I think we can dispense with counterrevolution, don't you?" smirks the derelict. In "Tesseract" the world awakes to find that a titanic hooked bauble hangs from the sky. A soldier volunteers to get his lip caught on the thing, and gets dragged into a hyperdimensional fluorescence of clarity and cures. But these do not translate back to his own world—when he returns, he finds himself holding a dense stone and talking gibberish. In "Can We Please Move On?" human expressions finally turn around and refuse to cooperate with people's stupid reactions.

Alan Rouch meanwhile, living in a treehouse in Lint's yard, invented the appalling "craw wafers," crackers made from flaked lobster shell. He had become disenchanted with the pulp world and when he declared that "the only new tale is a leopard in love with baloney," Lint wrote the story "Baloney Leopard," in which a colossal leopard attacks a bunch of Mars colonists and, alarmingly, will not be bought off with offers of baloney.

"Brokenhearted or pigheaded?" the colonists ask. "You can't be both."

"Oh yeah?" the leopard roars. "Watch me."

Though trash by anybody's standards, the story proved to be the first of a loose series including "Consolation Hedgehog" and "The Jarkman," collected in the slender volume *I Eat Fog* (Furtive Labors, 1962), Lint's belated fulfillment of his Rodence contract.

"We go look at the ocean," Lint wrote to Hemingway, who was on his last legs in Idaho and was still baffled as to who Lint was. "Surfers stick to its surface like black insects," said Lint. And this set off an image of upper-dimensional beings stuck to our dimensional surface and spinning a hyperthick snare that manifests as a

3D arachnid form. Lint's novel *Turn Me into a Parrot* is basically a domestic bug-hunt made apocalyptic with meaning. Readers would later recite the unnecessarily precise exchange in which Bobbi Watts warns Lucius Arlen of a spider in the house:

> "The little spirit is nocturnal, will invade the bathroom. The uncertainty is bothering you."
>
> "It was imposed by you."
>
> "I executed the feeling."
>
> "That's what I mean. What's the score with you, man?"
>
> "Well I found out that people are doing their own feelings all the time and this is my answer."
>
> "Making people jittery and nervous."
>
> "Everything in its place."

When a horrible larva is found in the cupboard, it seems the upper spider's snare has indeed caught something—a meaning as baffling as those in "Tesseract." Arlen roasts the semitransparent treasure for Sunday lunch and the meal is convivial. The central portion of the book consists of Watts having sex with a kind of customized cabinet containing many drawers and compartments. It becomes clear that this was the skeletal extrusion of a multidimensional chigger. Arlen becomes tired at these constant inconveniences and lodges a formal complaint to the upper bandwidths. The complaint is given a cursory reply. "The corner spindle of a spider, so what?"

The showdown with the bug is an exchange of challenges, Arlen winning over by questioning how a parrot can be changed into a parrot, or a human into a human—the demand cannot be carried out, of course, and the monster is sent back to the cold vast in medieval blasts of fire, hair and finality.

Parrot hit the shelves in 1962. The book's first line, "Spindly crutches descend upon the stairs, an insect bigger than you can handle," was only the latest from the creator of some of the most idiosyncratic first lines in pulp history, such as:

"I placed an atomic bomb in your eyebrow." ("The Fenchurch Conspiracy")

"How was I supposed to know barbwire was meant to make capture less funny?" ("Bill's Forebodings")

"Was it a giant gumdrop or a polished bible?" ("Last Beauty")

"False treasure is more colorful." (*The Phosphorus Tarot of Matchbooks*)

"There was a tiny zipper on the pearl." ("Broadway Crematoria")

"Doom was prearranged under the clenched heavens." ("The Jarkman")

"It's hard to determine, at the start, what you will be able to bear for a lifetime." (*The Man Who Gave Birth to His Arse*)

"I've never felt more wary than the day I visited Pobo the Clown." ("The Harrowing Squid")

"Strange destructive curios were floating over the city."
("Tesseract")

Lint's marriage was already in trouble due to his attempt to pass off a sleep crease as a glamorous knife-scar. His attempts to reimpose it by grabbing naps throughout the day put a strain on communication, and Lint's explanation of how he came by the scar was unnecessarily lurid, involving a shrieking nun and a meteor prophecy. As Lint continued the momentum of *Parrot* into the essays that would make up *Prepare to Learn*, his domestic life was falling apart around him. Madeline was outraged at Lint's borrowing one of her dresses for the delivery of *Parrot*, disbelieving his assertion that it was common practice. She later commented about her short time with Lint: "It's tough to sit at the table, listening to someone talk about a facsimile of a river replacing the river every alternate second. Friends dropped by for a beer and left believing their biceps were parasitic aliens. Hell, maybe they were. Maybe they were."

TEN

CATTY AND THE MAJOR

False cartoon ∘ *everything* ∘ *Can I see your skull, mister?* ∘ *the cat and the burnt guy* ∘ *exegesis* ∘ *journeyman reavers* ∘ *the Kecksburg Testicle* ∘ *hit and run* ∘ *casting out the self* ∘ *Herzog breakdown*

When NBC cancelled *Rocky and Bullwinkle* in 1964, they filled the slot temporarily with *Achtung Alligator* and began casting about for a long-term replacement—they wanted a zany but harmless new cartoon for the after-school slot. Alan Rouch had begun working as an assistant script editor at NBC and mentioned Lint's name to department head Arnie Waldheim. Waldheim was a fan and asked Lint to come in and discuss ideas.

Madeline was long gone, Rouch was now living in a tree house closer to the studio, and Lint was a lonely but driven man. He was startled by the invitation, as he had recently had a weird dream in which he was watching a strangely colored cartoon on

TV. A dark figure loomed up behind him and whispered: "That isn't a cartoon."

"What is it," Lint asked.

"It's a false cartoon."

During the meeting at the studio, Waldheim raved in detail about *Turn Me into a Parrot* and *Jelly Result*, and Lint was "charm itself," according to Rouch. Hired and surprised, Lint set about creating a product that would outreach the embellished vacuum of the average cartoon of the time. Television historians have since described *Catty and the Major* as "a wholesale defect."

Lint was very specific about how the characters should look. The Major's head was required to be "stained brown like a dead acorn or as though badly burned." Catty's leonine head looks mismatched with his body in a way that suggests he is wearing a massive rubber mask—when speaking, his mouth barely moves. Catty sometimes starts clicking his fingers and reciting his "crazy rhymes for schoolkids":

CATTY: What the hell is that bulging thing?
MAJOR: Can't you tell? It's everything.

The Major's voice is grating and low, his body apparently fragile, and he in fact seems to be in a constant state of dying. He often falls backward, "clacking," and lays inert for the remainder of the episode, wrecking any chance of frenetic action and complaining vaguely of an ache in his "rubies." In the notorious third episode, "Face It, Face It, Friend," the Major coughs up blood. Impressed, Catty tells the Major, "You are free!" The dissolution of illness is a step on the road to death's release. The Major bursts into bittersweet tears, the sky behind him spiraling like a hypnotic device. This shot continues for almost a full minute and has been blamed for provoking epileptic fits. Jamie Price of the Major-centered *C&M* fansite HereAreMyLastEverOrders.com has theorized that the Major's condition of "arrested death" is a symbol of nuclear threat in the age of "duck and cover."

In July 1965 the first two episodes were shown to a test audience of kids aged six to fourteen. The children's test cards point to a mixture of agitation, chastened terror, thoughtfulness and will to violence. One child emerged with the inquiry, "Will I die now?" Another approached an executive and asked, "Can I see your skull, mister?" God only knows how the show was allowed to proceed—Rouch later claimed that Lint agreed to make changes, but the four broadcast shows surpass any cartoon before or since in obscurely implied horror. In December 1965, households were treated to the strange banter of two creatures who stood mainly in a sort of abandoned gas station, moving in a distorted and freakish way, and flickering against muted color. Catty and the Major visited the drawling Lord Lazenby, drove a long purple car, and tried to dodge the terrifying Spike, a boulder-sized mace-head that ricochetted around in a hellish chaos of hazard, its out-of-control danger summoning a panicky blood-freeze in viewers. "I was so scared of that huge spike-ball," says fan David Shippers, "I locked myself in the bathroom and tried to suffocate myself with the dog." Other fans recount childhood nightmares in which they were pursued or otherwise molested by characters from the show. "Catty especially gave me a lot of grief," states Jamie Price. "He would press his face really hard against mine and very slowly open his mouth so that I could feel the working of his cartoon jaw. In the dream he was called 'Swan' but he was definitely Catty, for sure."

Some fans point with especial horror to the second episode, "Soon Antiques," in which the Major's lips begin to droop and fall away like black wax. Investigating the problem, Catty finds the cause in Lord Lazenby's yard—a replica of the Major's head built from dead flies. Catty and the Major lift the curse by stuffing a doll with meat and "charging it up" in the spire of a cathedral. Then they set the doll loose upon Lazenby—it causes mayhem in his kitchen until its head is blasted away by a shotgun wielded by Lazenby's wife. The mutilated replica returns to its creators, chuckling horribly from half a face. Catty and the Major scream in unison, and the episode ends.

The show was at its most unsettling when the characters contemplated the suspect innards of false people, as they did in the fourth and last broadcast episode, "Mannequin Heart." Echoing the "false cartoon" of Lint's dream, this story featured the notion of a "false radio" or block of "solid plastic space" in which nothing can breathe. "It'll never be popular," comments Catty prophetically. He and the Major begin the episode in an echoing ruin at night, moving only to pick up and discard an occasional cockroach—their criteria for approval is unclear. Then the Major begins to glide slowly forward as though on invisible wheels, plunging into shadow. Catty later finds him scrutinizing the form of an armored man that is embedded in the factory wall. For the rest of the episode they dig out pieces from the belly of the man and try to identify what they have. A strange, slowed-down trumpet tune begins to play over the scene. The Major is looking avid. "It will help me," he says. The frantic end titles burst in and it becomes clear that the episode has concluded.

In December 1965 a child was reported as having belted his school principal around the face—the boy claimed that Catty and the Major had ordered him to "tenderize" the man in preparation for their impending visit. At the network, *C&M* had become known as "that show about the cat and the burnt guy." In January '66, *Catty and the Major* was canceled—whether due to audience horror or Catty's resemblance to Lippy the Lion (or both) is unclear.[6] But the show has remained a presence through the massive exegesis of its deeper meanings. Those who have specialized in the study of the "Catty 4" (the quartet of broadcast shows) have described an insidiously mounting horror, self-disclosing layers of suggestive meaning that point to ever darker motivations. Some have said the process becomes "intolerable." In Edward A. Clark's essay "Marching Orders: Imposed Authority in the Catty 4," it is suggested that the main characters are both normal people incarcerated behind cartoon masks that will not be still or silent: "A frame-by-frame analysis of the Catty 4 has revealed 482 incidents of some kind of structure, foreign shape or unnecessary graduation of color visible in the open mouth of the Major. About half of these may be attributed to film grain, tenth-generation degradation and other artefacts. The others might be glimpses of the Major's real face." *C&M* scholar Robin Lowman has gone further, isolating these "shapes and fluctuations" in the dark mouth of the Major and stringing them together in a magnified, grossly abstract sequence. This eight-second flurry of quantum foam, she claims, shows quite clearly a trembling human mouth saying "Locked in, help, oh they have maimed me. No more, you'll take me out, say it."

There was a sensation in the *C&M* world in 1996 when Thomas Moorer isolated a single frame in episode 3 in which, in the tradition of cartoons from *Betty Boop* onward, the two characters appear naked for a single frame—the heads of both characters seem separate from the bodies as though jammed on like upturned buckets. Much of this analysis is summarized in Tatyana Koryagina's "Degraded Image Quality in the Catty 4: Toon Rot and Slipping Masks."

Many *C&M* studies concentrate on the relationship between the two protagonists. Den Hastert's "Death as a Friend in *Catty and the Major*" describes Catty as a kind of capering Reaper, carrying the ailing Major endlessly into his good night. Hestert (who famously authored "Gay Porn Color Schemes in Ernie & Bert" with its coining of "faded stock confusion syndrome") posits the notion that Catty and the Major are some sort of "champions," though his reasoning is muddled and refers repeatedly to another show called *Beany's Flight,* which apparently does not exist. In "Sediment of Cartoon in the Real World: The Major Crosses Over," Jeffrey Brzozowski describes a dream in which he finds "toon dust" in the corners of a room illuminated by a TV on which episode 4 is airing. The episode is slightly different from the one familiar to *C&M* fanatics, in that the Major actually dies and a tidal wave of grief engulfs the network. The toon ash burns like Hiroshima dust. After Brzozowski's essay an entire subcult of *C&M* dream literature sprang up on websites such as FalseCartoon.com and CattyWasntCatty.com.

There is conflict among *C&M* cultists regarding the relative value of the Catty 4 and the several unproduced teleplays—indeed, the four broadcast episodes are viewed very like the four gospels, to the apocrypha of the unbroadcast scripts. The most hard-line of the former are those who adhere to episode 1 ("Blame") as the be-all and end-all of *C&M* exegesis and express mortified disgust at the "soft" end of the discourse (Catty dreamers). "Blame" and its very slow yet apparently undodgeable flying fish is an odd episode but the scripts and sketches for the uncompleted shows make the aired adventures look bland indeed. Witness the story entitled "Satisfaction Replica," in which Catty beats the Major like a cur for making a discovery. The Major has found Spike's home, a "reaver hall" that shunts intersecting razor blades across its space, dicing intruders. The episode also introduces us to the Journeyman Reavers, people who worship the alien Spike. The tale has the airless quality of a delirium nightmare. Another unproduced script ("Untitled Catty script 3") shows us Catty holding the Major down and using a tire pump to inflate the side of his neck, then bringing an unidentified contraption to bear on it and drawing out a greenish fluid. This is all that happens in the proposed episode.

Lint himself became aware of the show's cult status in the late eighties and his only remark about it was, "I should have aimed higher." He never had time for those who traded in tenth-generation pirate editions of the four and was bemused at the existence of ritualized parties at which the shows were projected upon two chosen revelers who must conform to the characters' movements behind the Technicolor flush. Lint's memories of 1965 were tainted by the events surrounding the removal of his right testicle—it had swollen to the size of an Irish heart and Lint had visited a specialist in Westmoreland County, Pennsylvania, for the operation. But he became scared at the last minute, stealing a gun from a child and climbing onto the roof of a fire station. The resultant seige, shooting of Lint with a tranquilizer dart, and efficient surgery while cops tipped their hats back to laugh is one of the strangest incidents in Lint's life. A giant replica of Lint's ball now sits atop the Kecksburg fire house and many Lint fans make the pilgrimage there each year.

Lint was not surprised in early 1966 when *Catty* was wrenched off the air, and was already heavily involved in other projects, *Prepare to Learn* foremost among them. But in 1965–66 he was also distracted by obscure developments in the world of Cameo Herzog. Herzog was still based in New York, he and Lint corresponding only through an exchange of theoretical SF articles in *Bloody Fantastic Idea* magazine. But many have theorized that a hit-and-run incident in the street outside Lint's home was the work of Herzog and Dean Rodence, whom Lint swore to seeing all aglee in the passenger seat of the oncoming truck. "My arm broke under the wheel," wrote Lint of the incident. "It didn't sound like celery, which surprised me. It sounded like the bone-conducted thump of a marrow when you knock it against the counter. And you do."

Yet it seems Herzog was on the East Coast at this time, as several of his journalistic colleagues have attested to the florid breakdown he suffered in the lobby of the New York Public Library.

Caul Pin, the eccentric old Brit who would become notorious for his failed "Earth Sandwich" project, witnessed Herzog's convulsions. "It wasn't very practical," he says today. "He looked like a sort of convulsing ghoul. There was something so fundamentally spooky about the fit. But the finality was like sudden attention for him, I suppose. He was saying things like, 'I have clattered a thousand talents on the concrete through my frosty correctness and loved it! I am fattening the palmed coin as we are taught we should! I will not be attacked by some beefy idiot, or skeletons cleansed by God in the silvery world!' Something along those lines anyway. No one's more conspicuous than a man who's awoken from a lifetime of imaginary authenticities."

It seems that the source of Herzog's grief was his feud with Lint in the pages of *Bloody Fantastic Idea*. In an interview with the magazine, Lint had spun the notion that since crustaceans were skeletons containing meat and mammals were meat containing skeletons, then since the bones of human beings enclosed organs and marrow, humans were in fact crustaceans. In a subsequent issue Herzog countered that calcium traces in organs and marrow technically constituted a central bone system and that we were mammals after all. Impressed, Lint agreed. Taken by surprise, Herzog was simply unable to accept this turn of events.

A week after the library incident Herzog showed up in a meat market, running amok with some kind of rubber hose until cornered by police. Lint was in town to deliver half of *Prepare* and Caul Pin collared the sundressed author in the street, apprising him of the situation. Lint soon found himself at the seige scene insisting through a megaphone that Herzog was indeed wrong— within calcium were atomic particulates of carbon molecules and so on. Privately Lint was asking the cops why they didn't just use a tranquilizer dart on the bastard—"That's what they did with me."

Herzog gave himself up, his hose was confiscated, and he was led away swearing revenge. There is newsreel footage of his turbulent arrest, Herzog throwing panic at the camera. Glimpses of Lint looking on show him wearing some sort of bouffant daisy-patterned Montgomery Ward number with fitted bodice and full shirred skirt with an attached nylon petticoat. The further Herzog's career fell behind, the more strident his public claims became. While on parole he wrote several letters to the *Boston*

Globe declaring that Lint was a "rogue maniac" published only through criminal indulgence. "Shoot me if I ever write like that."

When Herzog's body was found a year later, his forehead containing a 9mm Parabellum slug, Lint was hauled in as the key suspect. But his surprised laughter upon hearing of the incident was so clearly honest, the police felt foolish (and reportedly "soiled") in holding him.

ELEVEN

"DEBATE THIS, YOU MOTHER" — SMASHING THE READER IN PREPARE TO LEARN

Absorbing all consequence ∘ Vacuum as Policy ∘ hyperlife ∘
too many novelties in his nobility ∘ America Immaculata ∘ pragments ∘
honored and scorned ∘ Paradox results from artificial boundaries

In 1966 Lint lowered what he called his "flesh stylus" onto the world and started laughing. He knew an author was exempt from mercy and bore this in mind to bluff-call and bring plain all potential and unspoken dangers in his path. "Art is one of those sure scapegoats," he told me in 1992, "absorbing all consequence with only mild surprise. But in a dull vacuum it's yet human nature to try striking a match." *Prepare to Learn* is a fierce environment of hurtling ideas like blurred paintballs from every direction, demands expounded in a hundred ways and justice expressed through easy mischief. The tradition of different explanations given by each rebel—that was a galling art, almost lost.

Prepare had a sort of shark jaw structure, new barbs folding forward as the previous were spent. Lint later said the book was "as simple as a scalpel" and knew its fate was to be ignored in the tradition of Algren's *Nonconformity*. "My clenched assertions do me no favors," he admitted and in retrospect critics have accused Lint of "fiending for pariah status." Some of it is very tough going, as when he declares, "An earwig's progeny will not grieve."

"For less than a single sentence," says Bojinka P. Richardson today, "it resembles the gray blocks of archetypal opinion, then takes a slight turn and leads you into what you realize too late is the diatribe of an ailing moron who spends his time eating hay and, perhaps, living human flesh." Not all critics are so damning. Mac Baginski claimed that, upon opening the book, a "blast of merit" burned the eyebrows from his face.[7] "But it was hardly a manual of forbearance."

"Civilization is the agreement to have gaps between wars," Lint stated, describing a world for the belligerent and the forgetful. "A shelter of immense preoccupation keeps off reality. On the cusp of learning, you know humanity is about to be blindsided by celebrity again. As if Atlas cringes under a baseball. Our corner controversies will not be remembered."

Lint identified the media's Vacuum as Policy positioning which would later manifest in the "subsistence literature" of the eighties and, had he but known it, the early 2000s. "We make the bureaucrat and thus the atrocity."

There are three bits of fiction in *Prepare*, forming an A-frame for the caustic essays—these are the parable-like SF stories "Glove Begs for Skeleton," "Bloodbath at Feeding Time," and "The Kennel Is for You" (this last about a hotel of which each floor is located in a different year—creaking floors seem to foreshadow the structure's collapse into postmodernism but when it does fall the ruins are entirely real and present, and people are really hurt).

"Bloodbath at Feeding Time" begins with a consideration of sustenance. "The ideal sandwich contains both disease and medicine. There's a fraction of human life that is virus luggage. How electrifying to think that a pitiful waiter may nevertheless condemn us to a quick death."[8] Warming to his theme, Lint ponders poisons: "A poison can kill the living—what, then, of the opposite of a poison, and what will it do to the living?" This leads into the story of Dr. Hammurabi, the mad professor who measures the difference between dead and alive and, applying that measurement to his own life in the plus ratio, becomes "hyperalive": the drabbest circumstance sears the eye with psychochrome colors, movement is through an easy field of pellucidant blood, beset by ability. He later applies the same measurement to something dead, but toward the minus, making it "hyperdead": sand under the skin, waiting room dust, and thought by court notification never received. Inevitably it occurs to him to measure the difference between hyperdead and hyperalive, apply this to his own hyperlife in the plus ratio and thus becoming hyperalive to the second power. By the time he has reached hyperlife to the eighth power, he is a blinding magenta globe that ricochets around like a pinball. This entity appears at people's windows and delivers Lint-like diatribes about "the transferable heavens of dogma; propaganda with its strangely boring air of assumptive encouragement; standard-issue opinion as dull as a Caucasian's comeuppance—these and other items condemn us to a quick clean lifetime of casket bargains and undreamed innovation" and so on until people's heads explode in spectacular clouds of inky blood. "One must certainly break out of a corpse," Lint concludes, "these crackpot bonifaces."

"Bloodbath" is immediately followed by backup material in the form of the "Commemoration Intercourse" essay: "Any description of a great truth will reduce it, like describing a ship by its anchor. But even at a hint we're sent storming to our polarities with hands over our ears. Stubborness is not wise—it has no other qualities than itself. Stubborness is not wisdom or courage. Those who ignore the problem by means of a savior may realize that rather than the merely good shepherd, Yeshua ben Joseph was an individualistic asterisk of informed speculation, insulted by the company of sheep. There are too many novelties in his nobility— he will not do for the purpose of mental cowards. Corridor morning; work filigree into the coffee surface, you poor sap."

"'Commemoration Intercourse,'" marvels fan Simon Gilbert in *Parasite Regained Zine*. "How amazing was that. Lint just went totally off his tree."

"We are the slop of the divine," Lint observes in "Intercourse." "How many poems are in a hill? How many inequalities are in a celebration? Which amount of fanatics is like a beehive? For the mouth, grimaces are an entire philosophy. Reparation? Authority after the fact is no authority at all." At times Lint became unanchored from earth like a dervish.

Many have stated a view on Lint's "unresolved anger issues." After the publication of *Prepare*, eleven psychiatrists wrote to Lint offering their services as a result of reading the sentence "Plants grow in retaliation to external stimuli." Rouch says that Lint was in fine spirits at the time of writing the book. "He gave people presents and was generally very friendly, though it was the kind of aggressive affability that was just a step away from biting your nose."

In "The Horror of Opulence" Lint was already preshadowing his *Easy Prophecy* visions: "Responses link like paper monkeys, losing all power. America will see an age of liberation—but it will be a liberation stripped of all content. *America Immaculata*."

Themes in "Opulence" were picked up in the penultimate story, another fiction, "Glove Begs for Skeleton," in which an administration imprisons its people in the comfort of gold robots and need do nothing more. Care became wiring and anti-inflammatory drugs. A needle-sharp nose, a screwdriver neck, something cold and perfectly tooled—for the days the inhabitant took to starve and beyond, it was a fine item and on the outside there was no change from one with a live inhabitant and a dead one (recalling Lint's rebuttal to Schrödinger, "The cat does know the difference"). Later the administration discovers it needn't have the robots really made of gold, nor need they really function. Soon leaden and untooled, these small tombs were cheap and easy. A man placed in an old-style case with functioning limbs wanders out into the arid landscape, collecting plain gut and shells out of vestigial curiosity. The pattern he apprehends in the clinking shells is clear, and made clearer by a kind of quartz *Zohar* he finds in an abandoned bunker. It is inscribed with warnings against a future that even their author did not truly believe would arrive: "The horror of opulence is the lack outside of it in space, before and after it in time, within it in mind and morality." The man spends days reading the ancient stack. "Preacher-dead and suspicious of questions, a government may at one moment appear to be

an orifice of a fuzzy fly, the next an ordinary fashion designer trying on a platitude, or a highwayman, or an unexceptional night. Yet
when you approach it, it resembles nothing so much as a dry toxic
husk in faded elephant sleeves." And "Simplistic geologists pray
for causation. The angelic tooth is offering us a way forward, but
the obliteration offered by such a Darwinian tooth is not merciful.
What we will find is the deadline of our soul, forever extended." As
the man dries toward death, he scratches his own thoughts upon
the inside wall of his casing, knowing that these scratchings are
similar to thoughts, never to be seen by anyone. "I call home to language, love and the truth of looking humanity in the eye." His call
is not heard.

The last essay was a summing up. "I've established to my personal satisfaction that rifles feel obliged under cinematic expo-
sure. Has murder ever been patented? There's a cash cow."

In his final ever review of a Lint work, Cameo Herzog
described him as "a twist of chattering rags," "a devious eccentric
who has somewhere laid his hands upon a typewriter," and "on
the manifest as 'company clown.'"

"This book is liquidation stock from Lint's collapsed mind,"
stated Herzog with finality, and it is true that, though *Prepare* was
written in one flow, it comes across as a disparate collection of
chest-clearing rants.

"Lint called them 'pragments,'" says Caul Pin today. "I suppose because he couldn't be bothered to explain himself."

Wilson Herring wrote of Lint: "The kindest thing to think is
that he is a crackpot of shimmering principles," which seems
either a contemporary compliment or an insult ahead of its time.

"This is a craftsman at the top of his voice, who happens to
want to bury us in a steamy load of despairing and accurate words,"

wrote the respected *Washington Post* critic Simon Henwood. He concluded: "It is impossible to imagine what Jeff Lint will do next, but whatever it is it ought to be good." When Lint was seen naked riding a spaniel a few weeks later in Albuquerque, Henwood denied having read anything by Lint, or having written a review of anything by anybody at any time. "I'm just a corporal in the Royal Navy," he stated, quitting the *Post* all smiles.

Another reviewer described *Prepare* as merely "some sort of commotion."

"Between the dark of trouble and the light of disaster," said Lint, "we pass our days. And if this is our condition, it cannot be taken away. Paradox results from artificial boundaries. Experience can't be derailed."

Lint was too creative to be considered dangerous. But he was annoying. The book's cerebral convulsions yielded up what has regrettably come to be one of Lint's most often-quoted phrases: "The Id is a dude."

TWELVE

CARNAGIO

Lint Trek ∘ *originality still abhorred* ∘ *Consolation Playhouse* ∘ *carnagio* ∘
Thrown stones were once stars ∘ The Converse Bell ∘ *Now whatever you do
don't touch that one* ∘ The Coffin Was Labeled Benjy the Bear

By 1967 Alan Rouch was a script commissioner at NBC and felt
justified in asking Lint to create an episode for the second season
of *Star Trek.* He had previously tried to get Lint involved in the
Peace Kids Summerama Show and Lint himself had pitched an
idea for a Miss Marple–like series, *Interfering Old Hag.* But *Star
Trek* seemed a more likely fit for the vintage pulpeteer.

Lint's episode was at first entitled "Planet of Brittle
Understanding," later shortened to "Brittle Planet," and finally,
when he'd decided what it would be about, "The Encroaching
Threat." Due to the *Catty* debacle he was obliged to submit the
script under the pen name Fred Flick and delivered it in disguise
by dressing as a man.

In "The Encroaching Threat" the smug, unoriginal blandness aboard the *Enterprise* finally reaches such an unnatural pitch that it triggers an event horizon, heightening exponentially the vividness of everything else in the universe by way of compensation. The *Enterprise* itself is the one drifting bubble of gray in an exuberant hyperevolving fizz-scape of boundlessly creative fertility. An infinite supply of original ideas batter against the hull as the crew within stands grim and concerned. Kirk warns all aboard against looking outside for fear of infection. "Wipe that smirk off your face, mister!" he tells a cadet in a red top. All are agreed that the cosmos beyond must not be allowed to continue in such an excited condition, but how to reverse the effect?

When the cause of the singularity is explained to them by a kindly exposition alien, Spock suggests that they open the airlocks with a semipermeable containment field in place. By osmosis, material from the weaker environment will draw through the membrane into the stronger environment, while retaining artificial life-support. Kirk reluctantly agrees to allow a few minor ideas aboard from outside—a sacrifice necessary to equalize the pressure. Too late, a pop-eyed McCoy realizes that the stronger environment is outside, and the crew is sucked outward against the containment fields, which bulge dangerously into the polymesmeric exuberance of the universe at large.

Here Lint describes a series of hypervivid visuals to be superimposed over Kirk's sweating face—he undergoes a sort of *2001* Stargate experience unachievable by weekly television budgets of the time. McCoy sees the treacly release of enzymes in redemption orgies of polarity breakdown, all matter flushing with an eternal blush of realization. Spock, eyebrow raised, watches fiery loops reconnecting in escalating scales and asks himself in echoey

                         WILSON
                          (cont)
             and putting the ship at risk with
             your god-damn piety.

                          KIRK
             You button it mister!

                          SPOCK
             He's quite correct, Captain. In this
             and other instances your lack of
             flexibility has caused death and
             injury among your crewmen. Simple
             logic demands action appropraite
             to the exigent facts.

                          KIRK
             Are you questioning my command, Spock?

                          SPOCK
             No, Captain. Merely your ability to
             adapt swiftly to changing circumstances.
             Prejudice has dangerously narrowed
             your perceptions.

                          MCCOY
             You can't kiss the eager upturned face
             of a _fact_, Spock. But you wouldn't
             know that, being only half human.

                          SPOCK
             It is possible to kiss a fact, doctor.

                          CHEKOV
             I'd like to kiss _your_ facts,
             Doctor McCoy.

                          MCCOY
             For god's sake, Chekov, I'm a _doctor_, not a

                                                   /more/

A page from Lint's Star Trek *script.*

voice-over, "If you had an idea that was complexly ironic enough, could it become independently self-aware?" Scottie, with orthogonal schematic blossoms flurrying over his face, begins laughing and shouts that the ship can handle anything. Uhura calmly gives Kirk a week's notice, her thoughts elsewhere.

Kirk, newly infected with originality but still influenced by his military programming, devises a plan to empty himself of all ideas and switch off the containment field, firing himself into the endless fertility and shocking it into a momentary withdrawal— the only place it can withdraw is into the *Enterprise*, thus reversing the situation like a glove turned inside out. Then in the nick of time he would close the airlocks, thus trapping everything of interest within the ship. The *Enterprise* would then be placed into quarantine forever.

Of course, everyone else is also sucked into space when the containment field is terminated, their own inner life canceling out Kirk's attempt at sterility. The little bubble of blandness has been burst, the environment within absorbed into the richness at large. "My god," Kirk whispers before dissolving into crimson-gold fields of rippling paradise code, "what have I done?"

Upon reading the script, Gene Roddenberry is reputed to have said "This isn't prose, it's gnats in formation!" and Rouch recounted that for three hours Roddenberry was "unable to unfold his arms." Upon hearing of these responses, Lint felt more confident than ever that the episode would be the season's highlight, and Rouch was forced to describe in detail why he was mistaken.

But as Lint explained much later, the only problem he himself had with the never-filmed script was the description of events aboard the *Enterprise*. "Even when a story demands that a bunch of characters be boring and unimaginative," he would mourn, "I somehow end up making them interesting." Thus Kirk's sudden, frighteningly convulsive dancing in utter silence and Spock's constantly stated "wish to be laminated." For the duration of "The Encroaching Threat," the new character Chekov is said to be "flirting with McCoy"[9] and Sulu is repeatedly seen "lurking" near a doorway while "sinister theramin music" plays.

The one time Lint met Roddenberry he asked him where the drones' toilets were on the *Enterprise*, or if such a human need had been eliminated. Roddenberry thought Lint was asking for directions to the toilets on the Paramount lot and pointed the way, leaving Lint deflated. "Foiled by others' happy ignorance again," he said later.

But Lint was to find a great gasping release from the rigid strictures of television drama. Two or three times a year he would journey to New Mexico to "reground" himself and to visit his mother. It was on the train to Albuquerque that he met Bob Prince and Jane Boutwell, who had performed a radical minstrel/mime version of *Frankenstein* on the streets of Los Angeles. Lint admired the young couple's bravery and the authentic look of Bob's scars, which he discovered to be the result of a number of beatings received from passersby. The couple were committed to anarchist/pacifist principles and the idea that there should be no separation between art and life. Lint was flattered when they asked permission to perform a theatrical version of his story "Consolation Hedgehog," and he was soon writing plays for the newly christened Consolation Playhouse on Seventh and Central, Albuquerque. He also performed, painted sets and even cajoled some funding from Caul Pin, whom he had met through the

Herzog slaughterhouse incident. Young actors gravitated to this outpost of sixties experimental theater and found a group that believed in collective creation, where the most extreme interpretations were given reign. In the case of Lint's hairy texts this often meant a conservative toning-down of his directions, as when he stated that someone should "explode into fanning gore" or "say every word at once." (Lint was said to have given "the stage direction which cannot be pointed to.") But many times they tried, and the results were a spectacular and unceasing assault upon the front and sides of the audience's faces. Consolation's philosophy was that the audience should contribute to its own trauma. "I have high hopes of this device," wrote Lint. "Unhappiness replaces melodrama." The average performance in the tiny upstairs theater was like some boiler-room psychodrama designed to wring a confession. The tickets were said to be stamped from human tissue. The doors were locked and audience members, terrified that they would be asked to join in, were asked to join in. Ushers made up to look like zombies would shamble by with trays of liver. Dragged onstage, a quailing gran from the audience would be vise-gripped by an actor who seemed to be undergoing horribly violent convulsions, point blank and screaming. "Your mischievious remedies have smashed us all!" shrieks Alger Lattimore in *The Coffin Was Labeled Benjy the Bear*, as blood streams from his eyes. The Consolation style came to be known as *carnagio*, "the theater of collapse too long resisted." At the start of *The Ravaged Face of Saggy Einstein* the curtains opened to reveal a dozen rocket-launchers aimed at the audience. Black powder flumed into the seating area as an amplified voice stated "Cerebrospinal fluid is great for kids!"

"Rehearsals and exercise sessions were pretty tough," says Richard Thomas today. "We were set tasks to pretend to be anteaters and stuff. Dredge up hassles from our childhoods and paint it on our bellies, like that, then press it against the wall like a potato print. Leastways that's how *I* remember it."

"We were working a lot with lurch energy," says Bob Prince.

Lint encouraged individual actors to perform different plays at the same time during performances, so that one actor would mount the stage to enact *Born with a Double Skull* while his fellow actor might be working from *Make a Wish Piranha* and another from *Slave Labor for Lovers*—their interaction more closely resembled the chaos of real life than anything he could have scripted. "Many of you lost a darlin' during the war," states Jack at the start of *Blame the Mouth*, at which a patchwork donkey ran on shouting "There are too many imbeciles in the bucket!," the opening line of *Certainly You Will*. Lint loved these random intersections, and the ill-lit gasps and dreadful conclusions of the audience thrilled him. The theater was a realm of constant change and instant reaction, faster and more physical than the book world. He roped in the Unofficial Smile Group to play during some shows, drowning out the dialogue.

And he was happy to "grip the lavish old planks" himself. It is apparently true that during a free-form exercise in which Lint was asked to reexperience his emergence from the womb, he sprang up and started firing a gun. And he often came unstuck while winging it onstage, as in his cameo during *27 Workshy Slobs*. Boutwell takes up the story: "Lint went off into some sort of improv about red murder-blood on an ice floe or something, how that was real, but glory is reduced to altars. He kept trailing off and looking at the audience in silence, like he was expecting some sort of response." He finally got one when someone fired a flaming arrow into his right leg.

"Lint's pants burst into flames and he was shrieking, collapsing back and forth across the stage," Bob Prince described later in his autobiography *A Publicist at My Grave*. "Of course most of the audience thought it was part of the show, and were booing."

In the hospital, Lint reexamined his philosophy of stagecraft. "The modern musical should be more than a mere ceremony subject to diabolical ambience etc.," wrote Lint. "It should be subject to criminal suspicion and possible arrest." Thus in *The Riding on Luggage Show* critics were baffled by the indistinct image of a gaunt creature crouching in blasts of electric light. Was he injecting himself or playing a violin? "The harp was dripping with chromosomes, making the performance revolting," wrote Roland Harriman of the *Albuquerque Tribune*. "*Luggage* displays all the symptoms of an angular hell. And when I tried to leave, I found that they had childishly locked the doors."

"Respect is rarely acrobatic," said Ivy Rhyging in a review of *A Dog Arrives Altered, a Mistake in Scale*, "and with all their leaping these bastards show the audience none." Diren Grey's article on the Consolation experience was titled "My Lost Hours."

Of *Blame the Mouth* (later retitled *Blame the Moth*), in which the entire cast dies whimsically early, Debbie Oxenhandler wrote, "Lint's contempt shows through like the sun through clouds. There is no middle of the road to Damascus for this bastard." Other critics were less generous, as evidenced by Corney Lievense's description of *Moth* as a "fecal downpour" and the damning *Santa Fe Times* headline MOTH PLAYWRIGHT DESCRIBED AS "LONER."

Blame the Mouth/Moth was a chaotic production in which the hero, LeRoy, is blamed when everyone wakes up wearing monstrous costumes of, according to the aggrieved Police Chief, "kerosene-resistant velvet":

CHIEF: Don't worry about LeRoy. For all his posturing, he's still just a spider.
LEROY: It's true you know, I am a spider.
CAST: Join us, Chief—we need your strength!
CHIEF: Well, juxtaposition isn't much of an incentive. But I'll think about it.

The play was made quite famous by a headline misprint in *Variety* reading OBSCENE PLAY ATTRACTS MASSIVE CROW. Lint comforted the cast when audiences were hostile, saying that "Thrown stones were once stars."

"These kids are hot with hurry and hazard," he wrote under a pseudonym in the *Village Voice*. "Make way for a fab new generation, Grandad."

"When I see what I've done so far I'm too pleased to apologize," Lint wrote to Terry Southern, and set about creating his theatrical masterpiece *The Converse Bell*. At ten hours with one hectic, desperate interval, *Bell* was daunting and operatic, culminating in the crucifixion of Strobe Bricker (played by Jane Boutwell) on a street sign flashing WALK/DON'T WALK as blood sprayed from the theater's sprinkler system, drenching the audience. The troupe left Albuquerque behind, touring *Bell* and *Luggage* in LA and then settling at a new fire hazard on New York's West Forty-sixth Street. Lint, still largely based in California, was less involved with the Consolation Playhouse from here on in, writing only two more source works for them—*A Team Becomes Embers Together*, and the knockabout slapstick of *I'm Carnal, You're Mostly Made of Ham*. Lint would formally sever contact with the troupe in 1970 (when it became the Consolation Arts Lab), citing artistic differences and his belief in "the bitter strength of the densely rooted." Lost in the quagmire of sixties experimental theater, his plays were rarely performed after 1970, though in fact they have dated less than most fringe work from the period. In 1988 a new production of *The Coffin Was Labeled Benjy the Bear* was put on in London's Garrick Theatre. At that time in theaterland it was considered innovative—no matter what the subject of the play—to dress an entire cast in Nazi uniform, thus implying a heavy subtext in even the lightest fare. In the case of *Benjy the Bear* it had been originally stated that the characters were Nazis, but through the constant revision involved in Consolation's interpretative process, this detail had been dropped. So by the fashionable redressing of the 1988 production Lint's intended meaning was inadvertently reinstated. "Your mischievious remedies have smashed us all!" shrieks Alger Lattimore as blood streams from his eyes. "Mankind will become a rib cage atoll!"

THIRTEEN

"MY GOBLIN HELL"

Death of Agent Baines ∘ *three fifths of a mile in three months* ∘
vestigial tail ∘ Just One Honest Statement ∘ *sorcerer's apprentice* ∘
"Or the mosquito gets it" ∘ Dragons of Aggrazar

Lint's contract with Doubleday had an unexpected sting in the tail. It obligated Lint to produce some sort of sword-and-sorcery adventure, full of inconvenient elves and pompously abstruse wizards in the style of Tolkien, whose Hobbit books were hitting big in the sixties. When he learned of this Lint went to see his literary agent, Robert Baines, in New York, only to find the office locked and a strange, swarming thrum sounding from within. Baines was in an advanced state of decomposition, his office blasting with blowflies and methane gas, and still he was taking 15 percent of Lint's earnings—Lint was not to hear of the death during his own lifetime.

"I only had three months to spring it on them," Lint would later comment. "And I wasn't in any shape." His notes from the time give an indication of his state of mind: "I suppose, then, there's a procedure. Procedure will have its—what's the score here? have its—duplicate my car—face me and see—so, wizards? Wizards. I give up, what are they? my privates are lashed to a nightmare pig—America's blame-reflex, burning a hole in its pocket." Despair was evident in his choice of associates, Phil Silvers among them.

Through a mix-up *Rolling Stone* had offered Lint $500 to cover a Nevada martial arts show and he thought to use the time to break into the book. Apparently Lint drove into the hotel lobby in an explosion of glass and, stepping out, claimed to be "a fantastic bunny, with no reservation." Luckily he did have a reservation, as well as an expense account for the course of the festival. "The desert was made of sugar," he added with a laugh. Lint had become convinced that he had a vestigial tail in the middle of his face and, stung by his own heartbeats, settled into the hotel room for a brainstorm that lay the ground for his "Fantastic Lemon" experience of '73. The spiral catalog of his crimes roared down upon him like a mechanical shark, its tail a lash of full-spectrum agony—the scaly rainbow of human evils. Dogs dropped through the dimension playing cancerous harps. Satire traffic crossed the room, blasting papers off the mantel and generally mucking up his judgment. The next thing Lint was aware of was a delegation of thugs on his doorstep with a bedlam of accusations. When the hotel management asked him to confirm his name, Lint professed ignorance and tore down a strip of wallpaper to blow his nose. They roared him to the police precinct, where he gave his name as

Isaac Asimov and gazed upon the officers with glossy, drugged eyes. He was almost incoherently mellow and the only phone number he could offer them for confirmation was that of the festering Robert Baines. But on returning to the hotel he found the scrawled manuscript of *Just One Honest Statement There in the Hat, and Civilization Saved; A Fantasy.*

It seemed to be the story of a sorcerer's apprentice whose curt and hated master crashes through social custom while holding before him like a warding cross the justification that he is teaching everyone an arcane truth. In fact the so-called wizard is just an appalling old man and the lesson all must learn is to kick him away when he draws near. Passing through a small village, he remarks "I just stamped on the head of a caterpillar, I hope you won't despise me for it," before launching into a five-page mockery of the villagers' corn-prolonging prayer. In a return to the dimensional glimpses of *Jelly Result,* we see "a moment trailing behind him, revealing his machinations." "Bringing the cauldron isn't everything," he sneers at the apprentice.

They meet some sort of zombie and only the apprentice seems curious.

"What is it like, being dead?"

"Adequate for my needs," says the dead man, and then the wizard slashes a bucket of water over him for no reason, cackling like a bastard. Throughout the book the apprentice must repeatedly apologize for his master's dismal antics.

It is a life of forced limitation. When the apprentice suggests in young wonder that the royal castle must be majestic, the old man is dour and doubtful. "Heavy in ironbound marvels. But majestic? No. A few warriors glint on the doorstep, with spitting bumpers for eyeballs."

"They cry?"

"All the time."

At one point they encounter a real shaman and the apprentice asks him his future.

"Among rock I have foreseen dates," says the real sorcerer, standing before a slope of ciphered graphite. But before the shaman can make his predictions, the old man shoves him, knocking his head on the cliff and probably killing him.

"No fuss," says the old man as he leads the concerned apprentice away. "Your dainty biology will disintegrate, don't you worry. What they will find is a vapor of an abstract boy." The codger has stolen the wizard's grimoire and recites a page, at which a hanged silver creature rears from the floor amid crystal exertions of growth, water circulating in silent innards. Eight feet tall, the dream murders ten local innocents before buggering off again. The old man offers no apology to the townsfolk save to say complacently, "The meal of nature never ends."

Finally, the reputation of the old man precedes him and those he would bore evade him, crying: "Ringing in his throat, a reminiscence is minutes from emerging—let's get out of here! Avoid fellows like this who are merely vague approximations, yes, search out the real thing, gentlemen!"

When the two travelers meet a devil-worshiping cannibal, the fraudulent wizard tries to marry the boy off to him. The apprentice protests that there is no priest, merely an aura of pure evil. "The devil can perform a marriage," chides the old man. "It's like a captain at sea." The boy now heaves a sigh which runs the course of eight pages, a sigh so chambered and elaborate it contains whole fields of golden circuitry and contracting skin, motives purifying in the sun. The killing of the old man escalates into a vivid bacchanalia to which all the book's characters are invited, the three witches from chapter four cackling "Casserole his secrets, sisters!" as they boil the charlatan. Hands drizzle with blood.

In a sort of epilogue, the boy, now a sorcerer, opens a stream and points at its inner structure, cages and cages receding into infinity. In one of these cages is the old man. "This is not a striped suit—I'm reduced to a skeleton," calls the codger. The young sorcerer climbs down, releasing the now sad old man, and they proceed downward to visit hell. Observing a ceremony in "the blind sound church," they voice their suspicion of the priest:

"What's that hidden in his euphoria?"

"It looks exactly like a religious charlatan's earnest tension!"

Attacking everyone, they are happy at last. But the priest halts them, affronted, and orders them to kneel.

"Why would I want to occupy a god reddened with others' blood?" the boy asks.

The priest's appearance changes to that of a godhead. "You were meant to battle this beast." The boy is granted a glimpse of a dragon in a colored reach of tingling space. "Why did you waste your life?"

"Because there were absolutely no clear and uncontradicted instructions left for me," says the young sorcerer. "The system is almost totally unworkable." The young man realizes that his current happiness derives from his coincidentally attacking someone who truly deserves it, the proverbial needle in the haystack. He scribbles through the god with his sword, slashing it to pieces.

The thoroughly unpleasant aspect of the old man, the long frustration of the boy's progress and the bickering dialogue of

Lint's report on the 1968 Nevada Martial Arts Expo.

the two characters all serve to make *There in the Hat* a far cry from the sort of book where magic ructions are sacred. "I suppose I never will be right until I'm ready to leech wisdom from you, eh?" was not the sort of response required from a sorcerer's apprentice, in a genre book anyway. The elf-clotted landscape is populated with "impractical customs, politicians pointing where they're not going, guardians unflappably asleep and figments of your imagination."

A journal note at the end of the handwritten manuscript says: "Spent the morning peeling angels off the ceiling. At eleven I offered to explain why a lot of everyday stuff simply didn't apply to me, thinking no one could fail to be stirred by my oratory. Think again." Lint would type up this piss-poor attempt at dragon fantasy two weeks later and mail it to Doubleday, who published it under the title *Dragons of Aggrazar* in 1970. "Some jesters pray for reality," wrote Lint. "That book was as dumb as putting a belt round a bottle."

His report on the martial arts conference consisted of a line drawing of a honeysuckle.

FOURTEEN

HOLLYWOOD HACK

Banish m'Colleagues ○ The Gloom Is Blinding ○ *Fanny fire* ○ Kiss Me,
Mr. Patton ○ *mannered and epicene* ○ *ghost of corporate future* ○ *five curses*

Lint had always thought Hollywood impregnable to talent and in
the mid-sixties was still chiding Terry Southern for "selling out"
with the success of *Dr. Strangelove*. But Lint was hard up when
publishers such as Doubleday and NEL seemed briefly to develop
a taste for his earlier stories. It transpired that Doubleday had
begun reprinting his material with such exuberance because they
thought he was dead. This increased the shock when he appeared
in their offices wearing a dress, the Random-rejected *Banish
m'Colleagues* in hand.

Robert Sellers, a lowly subeditor at the time, confirms Lint's
odd belief that an author should unfailingly dress up as "some

kind of cheerleader" when submitting a manuscript. "He was huge, like an ageing boxer, and barely fit into the skirt. I sort of took pity on him. The chief editor wanted to kill him with a tubular chrome chair, he had it raised over his head. I thought Lint could do something marketable but *Colleagues* was about these wandering elephants and was maudlin at best."

Indeed *Banish m'Colleagues* frequently lapsed into verse, as in the "Send Serum Stop" chapter:

> *an elephant mended*
> *is a tusker befriended*
> *an elephant dead*
> *is as big as a shed*

Sellers encouraged Lint to bring in his next book, and was rewarded a week later with the manuscript of *Balloons Hear and Understand*, a piece of trash. Sellers suggested he try to option it to a picture company, and put Lint on to a friend at Columbia, who passed him on to Kenneth Turnour, an executive who happened to be a fan. He called Lint to tell him he had burned *Balloons* for the good of everyone, and Lint rushed around to the studio to strangle the reserved Englishman. "He didn't seem to know how to do it," Turnour said years later. "Instead of strangling my neck, he sort of grabbed me around the middle of my head, squeezing that. It surprised me, but it was hardly dangerous."

Turnour explained the movie business to the stubborn author and Lint seemed to be taking it aboard, but his first venture into pictures was the result of his stealing a camera from the studio. *The Gloom is Blinding*, an experimental short in which a blurred clown (played by a young Alan Alda) eats a chicken to the sound of "Green Onions" by Booker T and the MGs, caused Turnour to actually black out. Lint later took the reel with him to pitch meetings as proof that his inaugural leanings were purged. "I was convinced," stated Turnour, "that once his baroque tendencies were vented, he could produce a damned good screenplay."

Yet Lint's first real script was *Despair and the Human Condition*, in which two grizzled idiots sit at a tool-strewn workbench in a dim garage and talk intricate shite for ninety minutes. Behind them stands a pirate made entirely of wood except for one leg of living flesh. The dialogue between the two men proceeds incrementally:

MAN 1: I will exact vengeance, er, retaliation, is that the word?

MAN 2: Yes.

MAN 1: Retaliation. Your blood will…

MAN 2: Flow?

MAN 1: Flow, yes. Yes, all over. So, er, what do you reckon?

MAN 2: About what?

MAN 1: Retaliation, your injuries and so on.

MAN 2: Sounds like a plan—simple, direct, with passion and just cause. I'm in.

MAN 1: In, you bastard?

And so on. Upon receiving a first draft, the baffled but trusting Turnour insisted that Lint inject a science fiction element. Lint responded by garbing the three figures in space suits, the speaking duo with mirrored visors in place to increase the mystery, but the pirate's visor up so that all could understand it was a mere wooden buccaneer. "As for the live leg," Lint wrote to Terry Southern with a dawning pragmatism, "the loss is a bitter but unavoidable concession." Yet he alluded to the leg in crafty new dialogue for the masked figures:

> MAN 2: I don't like killer bees, and in the spirit of "do unto others," have never forced them upon acquaintances. Can you honestly say the same?
>
> MAN 1: Some things are added, others remain—like a live leg on a wooden body.

Lint's script specifies that at the end, the two speakers should flip their visors up to reveal the faces of grinning chimps, the camera sweeping from one chimp close-up to another while the sound track provides a "revelatory blare of horns." The "pirate" spaceman effigy then bursts into flames and the ruddy conflagration finally freeze-frames behind slowly rising credits and Sinatra's elegiac "It Was a Very Good Year."

Turnour knew the script as a whole was a nonstarter but spotted an angle—Columbia was working up a screen version of *Funny Girl*, a stage musical about comedic showgirl Fanny Brice. He saw that Lint's gift for imagery could be adapted and suggested the burning effigy setup to director William Wyler. A showroom of mannequins would burn, *House of Wax*–style. "The Brice screenplay was still clunky, stagey. They wanted to make it more cinematic—and this was the perfect solution. It dramatized visually the obliterative exploitation of Brice's and other women's bodies. It was stark, horrific, unforgettable. We handed it to Wyler on a plate." The blistering firestorm was to form the centerpiece of the movie while being presaged by intense nightmares that plague Brice throughout, the hellish inferno even segueing ominously in and out as she sings "Don't Rain on My Parade." Lint also suggested that the wooden Nicky Arnstein (played by Omar Sharif) should begin "clacking his jaws and jangling like a puppet" while laughing demonically at the end of the "You Are a Woman" scene. Wyler drew the line. He had never really understood the idea and finally threw it out altogether. Today the film looks dated, and the only remaining glimpse of the "Fanny fire" can be seen in some prints of the opening scene in the Ziegfield Theatre where Streisand stops at a mirror to say "Hello, gorgeous" as phantom flames rage behind her reflection.

By the time of *Funny Girl*'s release in 1968, however, Lint was already working on two major screenplays. This had come about by his taking credit for *Barbarella* and everything else Terry Southern had ever done and by never mentioning his very real connection with *Catty and the Major*. The first and biggest project was his screenplay for a biopic of General George S. Patton, focusing on his military career commanding troops in North Africa, Sicily and France during World War II.

Kiss Me, Mr. Patton was a sprawling work full of detail and incredible set pieces. Lint had been fascinated by the antics of J. Edgar Hoover in *Foggy Hen*, the much-pirated home movie in which Hoover croaks to camera for three long hours, constantly repeating the words "I feel funny. Let's go and play." He wanted to bring a similar sense of precocious inner life to Patton, and wrote him as a fanciful tyrant who wears live otter boots, stands up in moving jeeps, and often walks about naked except for a barrel held up with braces. He keeps lurching during parades as though about to topple, but always catching himself at the last moment with a loud burst of laughter. He kills a monkey and makes an impromptu medal out of its nose. As he sits at the sewing machine, flushed and energetic, he shouts above the rattle of stitching, "This'll give Rommel something to think about." When he threatens to shoot a soldier in the hospital for refusing to get to the front and fight, the soldier begins larking about, fellating the gun barrel and generally acting the bender. Patton begins to snigger, unable to maintain his stony front.

Lint was told that the title role was to be played by George C. Scott and soon began modeling the part around the actor's craggy features and raspy, distinctive voice. Lint admired Scott and the two got on well. A man of robust humor, Scott even agreed with Lint's insistence that Patton should always look "boggle-eyed" and a pair of prosthetic eyes were created. Screen tests still exist of Scott barking orders in the strange lenses but the notion was ultimately abandoned due to a coincidental and striking resemblance to Richard Nixon. Scott nearly ruptured himself laughing about the scene in which Patton mutters for eleven minutes on the joys of being a "beaver magnet"—Patton finally mumbles into incoherence, trails off and is left staring into empty air for another eight minutes of complete silence.

"The first half of the movie," Terry Southern later commented, "could be interpreted in so many different ways that the implications really went over the heads of the studio boys. After the tank-dressing scene, though—which was like something straight out of the Consolation Playhouse—the whole thing just flies off the living handle." This scene, based on the "well-dressing" tradition of rural England, has the troops covering the M4 Shermans with flowers and fruits in a celebration of nature's bounty. Patton then suggests that the tanks should be disguised as gigantic otters. The size would also cause pilots to misjudge their altitude and ascend, he reasons. Karl Malden's performance as Bradley would have been well served had he been allowed to shout Lint's dialogue into the field telephone as the bombs exploded around him: "I injected the general's sausages this morning and am flabbergasted at the slow spread of the poison! What the hell did you send me—lemonade?"

The spectacular "Dance of the Tiger Tanks" which Lint envisaged as a finale, their balletic maneuvers viewed from above as Strauss's *Tales from the Vienna Woods* plays and Patton's gritty voice-over remarks that he's "bored with everything," can now only be imagined. Upon reading the script, director Franklin J. Schaffner is reputed to have placed it behind his car and reversed carefully over it, rubbernecking backward in silence during the procedure. The movie was rewritten from scratch by Francis Ford Coppola and Edmund H. North, the title shortened simply to *Patton*. The only Lint idea that survived was Patton standing up in the moving jeep, but with all hemorrhoid references excised, his behavior was rendered meaningless.

At the time of the movie's release in 1970, Lint was bidding farewell to another project. He had been instantly ejected from Kubrick's *2001* team when he suggested that the Starchild should have "fangs" and, coming straight off *Patton* and the previous disaster of his *Star Trek* episode, Lint wanted to attempt something classical, mannered and epicene. *Frightful Murder at Hampton Place* was a murder mystery set in an English stately home, all tennis and dinner parties. Intrigue, dispatch and disappearance are interwoven with clever dialogue and ice-cool observation. Mr. Singleton Haft calls to take tea with his sometime friend Lord "Bumpy" Bumperton and other guests. Lord Bumperton remarks upon the apparent disappearance of his daughter and, though all are suspect, they are more concerned with clever chat.

"Pies exist to provide a mystery that may be quickly solved and then thrown aside in anger," says Bumperton.

"I think you and I have quite different experiences when it comes to pies, Bumpy," quips Haft. "I love 'em, and push my nose through 'em like a snowplow."

The vicar chides him, threatening eternal torment in Hades.

"Hell again?" Haft remarks to the vicar. "This religion of yours is a firetrap."

Frightful Murder at Hampton Place is a masterpiece of Firbankian manners, and when Lint signed it away to meet his alimony, it was with a jaded foreknowledge. Totally rewritten at MGM and relocated to contemporary New York, the movie was released as *Shaft* in 1971.

Lint was by now utterly embittered with the movie industry and returned to hurling sarcastic, holier-than-thou gibes at Terry Southern. The final blow was the complete eradication of his dialogue work for Brando in *The Nightcomers*. Brando was supposed to stand in the garden and mumble "There's a peach in the way— my path is blocked. Hey, look at it. Love me, love me." Brando, famous for muffing his lines, ad-libbed an approximation that included the half-whispered statement, "Five curses I lay on thee—lice, failure, leprosy, ambition...and the worst of these is a marrow-deep complacency in regard to our political so-called leaders." Ironically, it was the political tone of this remark that soured the studios on Lint's screenwriting. The scene was removed and Lint quit movie-writing forever. It had been a sorry episode. Rather than a keen mind in high gear, his movie phase shows a creative force utterly muddled and compromised. Lint knew he needed to return to the book, and it was with a blast of fact-based truculence that he did so.

FIFTEEN

RIGOR MORTIS: LINT'S JFK BOOK

Ingersoll ∘ *Magic Bullet* ∘ *accident or frivolity* ∘ *Flaming Energy Clown* ∘
Umbrella man ∘ *festival of sadness* ∘ *knife attack*

Lint had touched upon the subject of presidential assassination in his story "The State of the Union Earful," an alternate history tale in which Robert G. Ingersoll agreed to keep his beliefs to himself and so was allowed the governorship of the state of Illinois and went on to become president. The story follows the preparations of an assassin in parallel with Ingersoll imploding with guilt and self-hatred, as he senses a swirling black pit at his center. Finally Ingersoll begins to physically implode during a public appearance, his center rushing backward into darkness even as the assassin's bullet approaches. Lint then shows us the screaming soul of the president tearing through infernal dimensions, the tardy bullet forever pursuing him.[10]

Rigor Mortis uses the suspicion helix of the JFK murder as a grand staircase by which Lint enters political discourse wearing only a training bra and a sort of seaweed bonnet. It got him into some scrapes that did nothing to improve his state of mind.

Lint loved the Magic Bullet theory, in which a single bullet had to swerve around to account for several wounds and thus discount the possibility of multiple shooters. "The argument resembles an invocation," he stated, and in *Rigor Mortis* coined the phrase he would repeat in the *Easy Prophecy* series: "America's make-believe is more dangerous than its reality."

Extending the Warren Commission's flight of fancy, Lint theorizes that the Magic Bullet was a ricochet from that fired by John Wilkes Booth at Lincoln in 1865. In outline, the bullet entered through Lincoln's left ear and emerged through his right eye, swerving out of Washington's Ford Theatre and heading north, felling politician Thomas D'Arcy McGee as he walked to his home on Sparks Street, Ottawa; ricocheting back along its original course, the bullet hit President James Garfield as he boarded a train at the Baltimore & Potomac railroad station, piercing his back, making a dramatic U-turn and piercing his back again, emerging in perfect condition to travel east across the Atlantic to create three separate wounds in King Umberto I of Italy and exiting the corpse at a right angle—in Buffalo the bullet knicked off a button of President McKinley's vestcoat, then made a 360-degree turn and entered McKinley's stomach, continuing east again to Finland, where it wounded Russian governor general Bobrikov in the stomach before circling back to pass through his neck at an angle which put it on course for the east coast of America, slamming into Theodore Roosevelt's chest, where its path was slightly diverted by a metal glasses case and slowed by the fifty-page speech that Roosevelt had double-folded in his breast pocket—it left the unharmed ex-president, picking up speed until it had enough inertial force to penetrate the midriff of President Francisco Madero in Mexico City and ricochet northeast to take out King George of Greece in Salonica. Curving north to Sarajevo, the bullet hit the Archduchess Sofia in the abdomen and Archduke Francis Ferdinand of Austria-Hungary close to the heart before spanging southwest to the Mexican town of Chinameca where it looped through Emiliano Zapata, causing multiple wounds and continuing this spiral motion until its encounter with the sleeping Venustiano Carranza, president of Mexico—orbital inertia seems to have sent the bullet hurtling back across the Atlantic to Warsaw's Palace of Fine Arts, where it blew three distinct wounds in President Gabriel Narutowicz of Poland and spent around four years following Benito Mussolini, occasionally darting at him like a wasp but without any lasting harm until heading Stateside again, blasting through the abdomen of Mayor of Chicago Anton Cermak and injuring four other bystanders in Bayfront Park Miami, but missing Franklin D. Roosevelt entirely, turning left in midair and hurtling to Vienna, where it connected with Engelbert Dollfuss, chancellor of Austria. The ricochet pattern continued as the round crossed the pond again to the outskirts of Mexico City, where it bounced cleanly in and out of Leon Trotsky's skull, circling the globe to weave three wounds through Mahatma Gandhi and kill Liaquat Ali Khan, first prime minister of Pakistan, in Rawalpindi; narrowly missing Harry S. Truman in Washington, it fatally wounded Anastasio Somoza, president of Nicaragua, Carlos Castillo Armas, president of Guatemala, and Prime Minister Solomon Bandaranaike outside

Lint's Magic Bullet (from Rigor Mortis).

his home in Sri Lanka—then set a course for the face of Dr.
Hendrik Verwoerd, prime minister of South Africa, where it was
not slow in entering his right cheek, emerging again and entering
his right ear, but failing to kill Verwoerd, though upping the
wound count the following year with the death of Patrice
Lumumba, former premier of the Congo in Katanga in the former
Belgian Congo, the bullet entering Lumumba and two of his former ministers so many times that they appeared to have been
mowed down by a CIA-appointed firing squad. The bullet made its
way to Jackson, Mississippi, hitting Medgar Evers in the back,
curving eastward to ricochet wildly around South Vietnam during
the U.S.-instigated coup against President Ngo Dinh Diem and his
brother Ngo Dinh Nhu, leaving them dead and bouncing west to
Texas where only twenty days later it entered Kennedy's back,
coursed through his upper chest, sloped upward, came out the
front of his neck, swerved right and down, struck Governor
Connally in the right of his back, pierced a lung, broke a rib,
moved downward to emerge from the governor's right chest,
turned right and plunged into the back of his right forearm, came
out the other side of the wrist, dodged sideways and ended its long
journey by burying itself in his left thigh, from which it emerged
later in near-pristine condition. At this point Lint claimed to fully
support Warren's theory that, though shot from behind, Kennedy
threw himself violently backward out of "sheer cussedness."

Lint further claimed that Kennedy fired Allen Dulles after the
Bay of Pigs disaster with the words "Pilot the floor of things and
stretch like a caterpillar, Allen." He also stated that Kennedy
named one of his dogs Stingray Hernia, that he told Richard
Bissell "Don't worry, I'm just a charismatic cloud" when firing

him, and that he asked J. Edgar Hoover "Why so crafty?" and, turning to Bobby, answered his own question with "Perhaps he's tired of being tiny and goggle-eyed, eh?" at which the brothers exploded into sniggery laughter. Kennedy often gripped Hoover's cheeks and flapped them like pants pockets. On one occasion Kennedy is said to have upended a barrel of fat over Hoover's head and then kicked him down the stairs. Kennedy would flicker his eyelids rapidly when Hoover entered the room in order to give the little man's movements a visually "Chaplinesque" quality. In the face of such incidents, Lint claimed, "the Intelligence community became hostile to Kennedy."

"Who gave the order?" Lint asked, and dismissed the orders of authority as a nonsense: "When you see clearly you will see how commands have no real basis. They begin at a point in midair that happens to be occupied by a person."

But elsewhere in the book a handwritten note is reproduced, supposedly in LBJ's hand, which says: "An accident or frivolity must retire his ambitions. Gills work together—let's do the same. Love always, Lynny." Such flowery language doesn't sound like Johnson, however. Even as Mac Wallace and his team were moving into position on the morning of November 22, LBJ put it more succinctly to his mistress Madeleine Brown: "That goddamn fucking Irish mafia bastard Kennedy will never embarrass me again."

Even the conspirators' mistakes fed into the desired result. The term "rifle among Oswald's possessions" passed into the evidence and report despite the fact that it was an order, not an evidentiary observation.

Some of Lint's assertions are, though harmless, unsupported by anything but his own truss. He seemed to add a bunch of witnesses who didn't actually exist, such as the "Tiger Man" and Mr. Cracklehat, a high priest who had to be "sewn into his morality each morning." The Tiger Man appears to have begun as his name for marksman Billy Sol Estes, but then splits off to become a boss-eyed wondercat that capers cartoonlike through Lint's scenario. Another witness was simply called "the clown," and this chimera has taken on a life of its own in conspiracy circles to become known as the "Flaming Energy Clown." Lint claims this jug-eared performer was responsible for the killing of Officer Tippit on Tenth Street less than an hour after the Kennedy hit and that the clown turned himself in a week later. The story is that the clown's accomplice deliberately attracted cop attention by reckless driving and, upon being pulled over, signaled the clown to burst from the trunk with guns blazing. It seems the clown stated that the reason he had killed Tippit was the same reason he now came forward to confess it—that no one else had taken the responsibility. Commentators have opined that he was actually resentful at the lack of respect given clowns and that the attention hogged by the assassination earlier that afternoon was the final straw. Either way, this concealed evidence blows the Oswald case wide open. JFK investigator Kane Sommers has since presented evidence that the clown had performed regularly at Ruby's Carousel Club.

In the days before Oswald's intelligence links had been uncovered it was standard procedure to focus on the apparently tenuous connections between Oswald and the strange cast of possible intel personnel around him, such as small-fry spook David Ferrie, who had been training anti-Castro Cubans—possibly out of 544 Camp Street, an address used by ex-FBI man Guy Bannister and, on paper at least, by fourth gunman Lee Harvey Oswald.[11] Jim

Garrison had claimed there was a connection between Ferrie and Bannister, and Lint pinpointed the connection—Jim Garrison, who knew both men. In fact Lint has a wail of a time connecting the hapless New Orleans district attorney to everything, even suggesting that he might have been the clown who ran amok in the Dallas suburbs after the assassination.[12] Lint later explained in a series of letters to Neil Kourbelas of *Bellyful Zine*: "The authorities' attempt at creating a tamperproof reality from lies had already failed, but instead there was a mass of absurdities too confusing to navigate, which was just as effective. I thought I could make the whole structure sick to dying by injecting it with superior absurdities. Like anyone who wants to really make a case, I should have just stuck to the ballistics evidence." Lint had underestimated the extent to which the murder now dwelt in a compound dimension of real life and suspicion, and that whatever nonsense he threw at it would be taken up to further blur matters.

But a more compelling reason for turning strong light onto Garrison is that Lint himself was present that day in Dealey Plaza, sitting with the umbrella-phobic Cuban José Alvarez on the verge of the knoll. Lint had a black umbrella with him and at the time of the assassination was apparently telling Alvarez about Erik Satie and the composer's collection of over a hundred umbrellas, mostly unused and left in their wrapping. When his friend did not rise to the bait, Lint took up his umbrella and began pumping it open and closed, sniggering like a bastard. Losing patience with his taunts, Alvarez left Lint sitting on the curb. Lint's view of the fatal shot was obscured by his fooling with the umbrella and he only gradually noticed that something was amiss. Some conspiracy theorists misread the account (which Lint leaves until late in the

book) to mean that Lint was telling Alvarez about the gunman
Lucien Sarti, who fired the headshot from a few yards away at the
picket fence—Lint must therefore have been in on the conspiracy.
In fact Lint does seem to be one of the few people in the plaza who
was not overly surprised at the assassination, but this was more
through historical knowledge than complicity. Lint was a quick-
enough study to realize he was not a target.

It was almost a decade later that Lint himself came under
attack. "He was what these days would be called a free runner," says
Caul Pin today. "Attempting to cross whole cities by leaping from
rooftop to rooftop. It was his only exercise. Of course he was living
in suburban LA where there were quite a few open spaces, and he
had to really exercise his imagination to get a fair shake at it." Lint
would leap from actual buildings onto those he projected with his
mind's eye. "Naturally he went straight through the latter and
smashed himself up pretty badly, several times. And on each occasion he sent a detailed account of the incident to positive thinker
Norman Vincent Peale, claiming to be baffled by the outcome."

It was upon returning home after one of these mishaps that
Lint was pounced upon by onetime *Baffling Stories* editor Paul
Steinhauser, who lay in wait in the house and stabbed him twice
with a Boker carving knife, screaming with such incoherence that
Lint had to ask him sixteen times to repeat what he was saying.
Lint was wounded in the side and back, and as he lay bleeding, the
gaunt and bearded Steinhauser accused him of "turning me into
the Belly Guy." Lint confessed that he hadn't a clue what
Steinhauser was going on about and the ex-editor shrieked anew,
grabbing up the page proofs of *Rigor Mortis* and hurling them in
the air before throwing himself at Lint amid the paper snow.

"He said he would doom my torso to silence, which I thought was a great phrase at the time," writes Lint in *Arse*. "Movement in a household of death serves who, I wonder. Anyway, he stabbed me one more time, in the leg, and we both started getting bored because it was the same thing three times. And in my case, I had the pain on top of that. He went to a mirror, surveyed the elemental frenzy of his reflection, said 'Forty months every year, that's my motto,' then presumably thought he'd better go and have a shave. That was the end of it. I don't hold it against him. Narrowed to revenge, life points only one way, but at least it may wind up being of interest to more than one person."

But Lint was more affected by the incident than he thought. After a hospital stay he returned home and more or less stopped going out. "Dawn seemed carnivorous," he said later.

The packaging of *Rigor Mortis* inevitably yielded to sensationalism. The cover blurb screamed: "Earl Warren laughed if he saw a dog or a cat. This was the only time he ever moved his mouth. SHOULD HE HAVE BEEN PUT IN CHARGE OF THE KENNEDY COMMISSION?" In fact Warren often moved his lips when reading and, in defiance of advice, when standing near the gears of a combine.

Reader reaction was predictably useless. "Did he write the book or grow it in the trunk of a half-car in the yard?" asked Anthony Tangeman of the *New Yorker*, which Lint had once described as "the ecclesiastical newspaper of death-excellence."

One reader, his blood boiling, pulled at his own ear so hard that it sprang back into place with a noise like a whipcrack—he was dictating into a tape recorder at the time and an audio sample of the event[13] has become one of the most frequently downloaded files on the web, along with the exploding shark and Limbaugh stating a verified fact.

"Tens of thousands of dissolving motives make up the sunset," Lint wrote in his journal, but his own motivation was to return with a bang.

SIXTEEN

THE "FANTASTIC LEMON" EXPERIENCE

The Hours of Betty Carbon ∘ *Lint wedges* ∘ *C. H. Hinton* ∘
infinite intrusion ∘ *The Stupid Conversation* ∘ *unlikely at best* ∘
a new category of sight ∘ *going underground*

By 1973 Lint found himself in a strange position. In the literary world he was the head of a movement; was credited as the first author to steal Michael Moorcock's "Multiverse" idea; had coined the conspiracy term *dupe fatigue* in *Rigor Mortis*; and according to an (albeit incorrect) analysis by Stanley Spence of the *Philadelphia Inquirer*, had "made the people thereby so curious and so arrogant that they will never find humility enough to submit to a civil rule." Yet but for the occasional visit from a cleaner ("the spiders are blossoming under her care") he was subject to the irreplaceable zap of loneliness in his Fullerton home.

Lint was working on the never-completed *The Hours of Betty Carbon* in a house full of burnt dust, credit and worry. Caul Pin visited him at this time and found Lint bitter and agitated. Lint was saying: "It seems these bastards are bored with the flood of original ideas I—" and broke off, strangling the air before him as though confronted with a highway patrolman. He complained of having a migraine that was "an emptiness of flashing hell."

Though able-bodied, Lint became obsessed with placing ramps everywhere. Caul Pin again: "Jeff Lint was dedicated to putting ramps in front of everything, God knows why. But years later, many disabled people took him up as a sort of campaigning saint because they thought it was to do with access. While in fact I think he probably just liked approaching things on the slant." Lint spoke later about the beauty of the wedge and claimed that he had been "placing clues" about the town that could be "mentally collected and assembled together like Hinton cubes." Charles Howard Hinton, whose work formed the backbone of Edwin Abbott's earnings in the late nineteenth century, had publicized the memorizing of a cubic yard of one-inch cubes. Having memorized a block of space, it was then possible to place any object (mentally shrunk down if necessary) inside this space and feel exactly where it began, where it ended, what space it occupied, and what space it did not. You were then seeing in 3-D—the way a 4-D creature would see. It seems that Lint was attempting something similar with his Lint wedges. By memorizing each wedge-shaped piece of space and assembling them into a mental sphere in which samples of space from throughout the city were present, people could carry a "facet-map" in their head. An urban legend has grown up since that cabdrivers began to use the system and became so entranced with the contoured revolving gem in their minds that a sort of cult was spawned, and cabbies who drove into walls and through freeway barriers into whistling air were considered martyrs to the crystalline city.[14] This wedge experiment would lead Lint sideways into mind-map programming in the blood vessel–busting 1988 book *The Phosphorus Tarot of Matchbooks.*

But on May 15, 1973, this and other mental experiments seems to have culminated in what was a florid breakdown, a religious experience, a charming anecdote or a cosmic intervention for Lint. At this time he had been eating a lemon every day because, he said, he could no longer imagine the experience. He was distracted from his work on *Betty Carbon* one afternoon by the feeling of peculiar eternities—years in a minute he was staring at the blank page and when he finally turned to look at the room, an alien totem pole carved from angelskin coral and klieg marble had taken up residence. Around it hurtled feedback angels and battering photons, minds endless and dense irradiating the room. Cathedric creatures, entities in knots and tesseract nations defied the scale of the house with gem infinities. From the great beyond flapped a thousand demons on wings of cancer, dropping quicksilver bombshells.

For five days Lint lived amid the cognita inferna of proliferating dimensions. Gnostic nobs on the wall seemed like controls, which Lint manipulated without effect. Just to get to the kitchen he found he had to shoulder his way through blown-glass saints and the morphing emergence of fourth-dimensional limbs as "air cherries" that stretched and dwindled with only apparent randomness. Fifteen unseen creatures collided above his bed one night, smashing their brittle heads and crashing to the floor. Lint walked through fathoms of obsidian bedroom to find the light switch, hitting it to turn and see a plump animus struggling on the carpet, its semiformed face resembling that of Cameo Herzog. When Lint encouraged it to drink from a saucer of milk, the creature exploded into a hail of choking black dust.

"Of course, *Betty Carbon* was kicked in the pants," Lint explained in the autobiographical *The Man Who Gave Birth to His Arse*. "What I wrote then was a surrender to the bathysphere part of the human mind. Despite platitude universes beyond the door, I dwelt in squalls of unimaginable intensity. I was in the fully fledged moment. Happy and volatile, I roared through a labyrinth of bad gems." *Betty Carbon* had been intended as a follow-up to the forgettable *Sadly Disappointed*[15] but now, his mind a boiling chaos of supposition, Lint began work on *The Stupid Conversation*, in which the early character Lucius Arlen appears in regenerated form as Felix Arkwitch, charismatic bad boy of an occult assassin bureau, the Guild of Perfect Interruption. Able to shape-shift and given to appearing to his victims with flaming hair and "an erased face like a deviled egg," Arkwitch was the only character Lint was to return to with regularity, and this terrifying hero built up a following more sustained than that of the superficially similar Jack Marsden. While Marsden seemed to be walking around with a head full of gunpowder, Felix Arkwitch is the chemical interior of his own reasoning, set in motion across diagonal category landscapes with his eyes on the endlessness above. He walks invisible by "belonging to his own labyrinth." Jagged and tragic, he responds to threats by taking them inward and setting them to work. An inch of future divides him from apocalypse. "Wandering in the realm of souls leads you back to the world striped with the zing of golden death." Arkwitch is a white deathbed snake.

"Nothing ends enlightenment so quickly as a visit from the Jehovah's Witnesses," said Lint later. "There they were with the mummified voice of a survival god. The universe leaks bastards all over the place—I suppose it's natural some should get in here. When I looked back, the portal was curled up, shriveling like a time-lapse flower, and gone. A good ride while it lasted."

Marshall Hurk (who had bailed Lint out after the Nevada martial arts show debacle), remembers Lint showing up with a hectic look in his eyes: "The door rammed open and Lint hung in, laughing blood. He was undulating in the doorway like a dinghy trying to dock in high winds. I swear he was paler than an ambulance." A nest of static crowned his head as he explained his visions. "He stated that 'grace was scrambling over the walls,' which seems unlikely at best."

"Better men than you have been undone by this sort of soupy revelation," Hurk declared finally. "I diagnose excess of heaven. Cinders in the skull."

"Our mild conversation was interrupted by the crashing entrance of a falling seraphim," Lint recalled later, but Hurk remembered nothing of the kind.

In the visionary afterglow, Lint was still speculating on visual blips in the wallflow. "Fields seemed bizarrely flavored, succulent fire exploding in confusion, shapes reshuffling and making creepy lacunae in the sky."

Lint would be kicking the tires of the experience for years, and even used it retroactively to explain his unremembered transport to the West Coast in 1960. He was blessed with occasional flashbacks. "Twice a year things become jeweled, foreign with new windows."

But in *Arse* Lint described the experience primarily as one of regeneration. "I'd become distracted by image and career," said Lint, "something I'd never thought would happen. There's an old Persian saying, 'A flea won't be chained to an oar.' Don't make yourself conspicuous." Lint returned to his inner work, quietly producing a number of books throughout the seventies that would find their way onto the shelves up to ten years later. "I'll have plenty of time to be fashionable after I'm dead."

Lint never could explain to anyone what was so "fantastic" about the lemon.

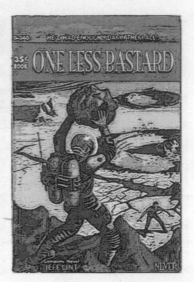

FURTIVE LABORS
science fiction

JEFF LINT
I EAT FOG

JEFF LINT
PREPARE
TO LEARN

Science Fiction

TURN ME

INTO A

PARROT

JEFF LINT

"The inept meanderings of a tragic mind."
- Cameo Herzog, author of I WILL MAKE YOU AN EXAMPLE

TOP: *Catty and the Major: coping mechanisms incarnate.*
MIDDLE: *The Major is already near death in episode 1.*
BOTTOM LEFT: *A curse doll returns, giving our heroes the heebie-jeebies.* BOTTOM RIGHT: *The Major's vortex of release. This long scene caused epileptic fits among viewers.*

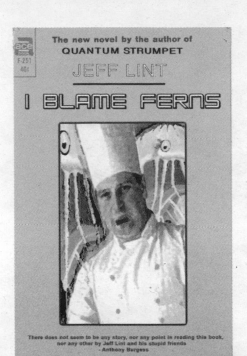

The inclusion of this apparently baffled chef on the cover of I Blame Ferns spoiled a major plot point for readers.

Lint proposed a pop-up edition of Rigor Mortis but was urged to be grateful for what he had.

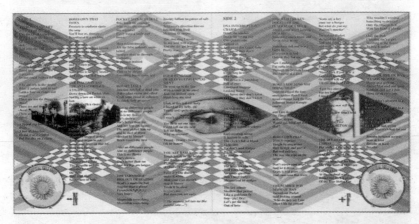

TOP: *Front and back
covers of* The Energy
Draining Church
Bazaar. CENTER: *Lyric
gatefold of* The Energy
Draining Church
Bazaar. BOTTOM: *Jeff
Lint at the time of* The
Energy Draining
Church Bazaar.

TOP LEFT: *The company-killing 9th issue of* The Caterer.
TOP RIGHT: *Jack Marsden freaks out.*
BOTTOM: *Part of the arduous goat diatribe.*

Dern House editions of the Arkwitch series.

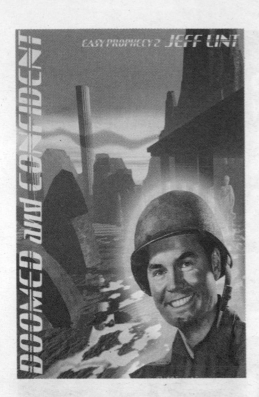

EASY PROPHECY 2 JEFF LINT

DOOMED AND CONFIDENT

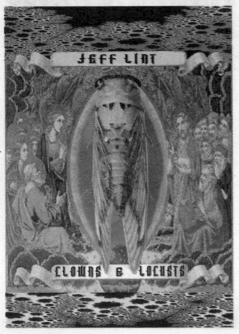

JEFF LINT

CLOWNS & LOCUSTS

SEVENTEEN

"LINT IS DEAD"

Felix Arkwitch ∘ *where an amateur can grin* ∘ *dog attack* ∘ *crown of gears* ∘
eye trumpet ∘ *into the minus?* ∘ *how about another one* ∘ *unscrambling*

After the Fantastic Lemon event came a year of black amazement, a season from the back of the head. Growing in identity, need exhausted, Lint lived in privacy and bathed in scorchers, producing and enjoying his time. But something in the air, and grapevine reports of the knife attack, resulted in a surge of bizarre rumors that Lint was dead and that the Lint from 1973 onward—or perhaps from 1965 when Herzog and Dean Rodence apparently ran him down with a truck—was not Lint but an imposter. Maybe a death-faked and surgically altered Cameo Herzog was attempting to hijack Lint's success or change his style by the most drastic method. Some pointed to Lint's pursuit of TV and comic projects as proof of a personality transplant. This ignores both his earlier work on *Catty and the Major* and the characteristic strangeness of the later misfires—certainly Herzog, who once described the sea as "immoderate," could not have produced these. But rumors of Alan Rouch's participation in *Sadly Disappointed* further confused the issue.

There was also a problem with the first edition of *Rigor Mortis*. The biographical notes on the back cover—with the by now inevitable photo of Lint kissing a tortoise—stated that Lint had died in 1972. The media, poised to praise him after his death, sprang in with lamentations that he had been tragically neglected by commercial enterprise and that it was baffling that his artistic genius had not been more appreciated. Their bitter embarrassment upon learning that he was still alive and open to their patronage drove a bigger wedge than ever between the media and Lint—they had no recourse but to pretend he did not exist at all. "So in terms of money, publicity, and ease of progress," Lint observed, "all remains the same."

But to his increasing fan base it was an engraved invitation to rampage across his works, pulling, as Lint put it, "inedible tubers of wild interpretation from my territory." The toughest of these tubers was the now recurring character of Felix Arkwitch, who appears in *The Stupid Conversation* (1974), *Fanatique* (1979), and *The Phosphorus Tarot of Matchbooks* (1988). This heaven-and-hell-frequenting antihero, who appears as a black ghost like an old suit, an arsenic-green mantisman or an urbane sculpture of gesturing ice, was theorized by many to be Lint's literary ghost uploaded into some creepy device and still producing after his demise. There were, some readers said, many hints in the text that

Lint was no longer around. Felix says at one point "Fancy going to the idiosyncratic nightmare of the pub?"—supposedly a standard Masonic remark upon the death of a brother. The entire first chapter of *Fanatique* was put through a cipher program to produce the phrase: "I whisper abaat nuffin." One fan pointed out that the word "dead" occurred thirty-eight times in *Matchbooks*. Others have countered that "sniggering" occurred more often than that, and that the two conditions were not compatible. Aurora Hurlburt wrote an article called "Jeff Lint: Dead and Sniggering" which refuted this view. Published in *Jellysump Zine*, it imparts great significance to the fact that Arkwitch escapes to the place "where an amateur can grin without attracting comment, where mudslides matter, where fingers tense and finally relax." Where else is this but the grave?

In 1969 Lint posed for a series of pictures that came to be known as the Savage Set. It shows Lint being attacked by a large dog in a field. The photos, taken by Jack Barnett to accompany a magazine article on the author, have attracted the attention of Lint theorists due to the fact that in later shots, a wound is clearly visible on his neck—a wound that was not visible in the early shots. The conclusion drawn was that Lint had been replaced by a doppelgänger halfway through the session. "The pictures were taken in a park down the road," Lint explained in an interview. "A dog attacked me, and the photographer decided it wouldn't be a bad idea to take a picture of the onslaught. The shots were pretty good—you can see the fear and panic in my eyes. And that's how I got the scar on my neck."

Other pictures of Lint show him frowning (apparently confused as to why he is being photographed)—many fans have remarked that the frown pattern on Lint's forehead resembles a crab, the symbol of reincarnation in Sumerian culture. Lint's forehead did resemble a crab when he frowned, but in Sumerian culture the crab symbolizes creativity. A photo appearing in *Rolling Stone* shows Rouch, Herzog, Terry Southern, Lint, Peter Van Metre and Marshall Hurk in Fugazzi's in 1953. Lint's sloping stance, actually the result of being struck several times by all five men just before the photo was taken, was identified as the ritualistic "mourning slump" adopted by the ancient Iscarii when a comrade fell in battle. Furthermore, if you place a mirror horizontally across the photograph, the six men look as though they are waist-deep in water.

Even the seemingly innocuous *Lint: A Collection* bore a bunch of clues. "A Collection" was seen as an allusion to "arse collection," British slang for a coroner's visit. The stories within include the suggestive "Imitation Panic" ("Have you worshiped the wrong core, brother?"), "I Would Have Spoken If There Was a Bounty" ("Who is the stranger pushing your cheeks inward so that your mouth purses like that of a fish? It is I! It is always I!") and "Soup in the Manger," in which a government department is set to work overlapping patterns of public complaint to design wallpaper—the result is "halloween rubbish; faded crimes." It was repeatedly rumored that Lint's gonzo article "Mashed Drug Mutants" had a subtext that was nothing to do with drugs, but Lint denied this. And the artwork has not escaped interpretation. Each of the twenty-eight stars on the cover represent one of Lint's mistakes, compounded by the large central picture of his face.

Literary groupie Cheryl Daly claimed to have slept with Lint and that he wore a black armband around his cock, a symbol of mourning in some cultures and a device to increase size in others. Other fans who have met Lint, especially later in his life, have claimed to have witnessed bizarre physical/metaphysical events that suggest that Lint could navigate between the worlds like Felix Arkwitch. Tom Hull relates a conversation he had with Lint in Santa Fe in 1987, at the end of which "his features shot into squares, receding at speed. Funny way to leave it."

Another theory in circulation was that Lint had been replaced by an alien in the sixties and this alien had come to believe its own cover story—the Fantastic Lemon transmissions were home-world attempts to reestablish contact. Thus the attention lavished by fans on the plot of his contribution to the short-lived *Incredibly Bitter Stories*, "Lipstick & Shells," in which aliens overtake Earth insidiously by infinitesimal drilling into our colors, changing them incrementally from within. "Our definitions will be changed from the core," writes Lint, "beginning with *anarchy* and *schizophrenia*." Dating from 1961, the story is said by some fans to be evidence of the alien Lint's screen memory going on the blink. "The Test of Crowns" has undergone similar scrutiny, containing as it does a crown full of gears that meddle with the mind, prodding it toward the appropriate. The crown happens to have been built by technicians working in the vanguard of execution, effectively inflicting the slowest death possible upon the state head.

In the realm of music, Lint seemed to offer further clues. While much of Lint's sixties work could be seen as a literary analog of pop psychedelia, he had drawn closer to mainstream flower culture in the late sixties with his collaboration on a strange, downbeat concept album, *The Energy Draining Church Bazaar*. This psychedelic epic was recorded with the Unofficial Smile

Group (later called Unsmile in its prog rock incarnation), part of the San Francisco scene but in 1969 already going to seed. Lint reenergized them for their last burst of authentic glory. In the style of album covers of the day, *Draining*'s cover is a seething mass of Technicolor images—these swirl around the figure of a younger Lint, wearing a crown and holding what appears to be a smashed marrow, but which many have seen as a parsnip, traditional wake food in some cultures. Rare copies of *Draining* bear an alternative cover on which Lint is shown to have a "living trumpet" (according to *J-Lint Zine*) growing from his right eye. This trumpet (or flower) has been called anything from "the lily of death" to "everyone's gumbo." Or was it a reference to Cameo Herzog's *Empty Trumpet* series? On the back cover, Lint stands off to the side of the four Smile members, a burning papier-mâché sculpture of the devil taped to his arse. Directly beneath him is a caption that reads: "Power remains in negative for an extremely long time."

The album tells the story of the Pocket Man (Lint himself?), who has dodged the "talent vaccine" given everyone in a future of registered thought and tear inspection. But his genius prevents him from participating and he grows lonely. At this point the album diverges into a dozen different strands, with songs like "Hydrogen Sheriff" and "The Number Nineteen Is Made of Wax" containing Lint's most opaque lyrics. "Stand back if you hear a gearshift in an egg," he warns. "Or no one will see you 'til the middle of Feb." In "The Pangolin and the Anteater Have a Fight" (nominated without any real hope as a new official theme song for San Francisco in 1984), a vision of the Pocket Man descends gigantically upon the gray world, flanked by quantum foam dolphins.

Gold dust for conspiracy theorists was a final coda that remembers the Pocket Man fondly, "Dead or Not, He Was Wearing Shades," and concludes by urging us to "Breathe between accusations at least." This final track contains the repeated refrain "Everything is pleasing to a hyena." Was this a reference to mass hysteria, fashion, the excitability of crowds? Who is the Hyena? Fans had endless fun with these questions.

Lint scholars sympathetic to the "Lint is dead" notion have frantically dissected the lyrics of the penultimate track, "The Delaware Christ." The words prove most compelling, however, when reversed—fans of Lint and of Unofficial Smile wore out multiple copies of *Draining* by dragging the vinyl backward, and the claim is that the band went to town with hidden messages. Reversing the lyric "You're ready but strict, baby / This isn't that kind of revolution," overattentive listeners have found the message "Legend anniversary, kill the driver! Ho! Ho!" Others hear the statement "He's angry and he's sorry. He's the driver. Herzog!" (An allusion to the hit-and-run of 1965?) In "Ignore Tesla," the invention of operative atoms and pioneer voltage is simultaneously exploited and scoffed at by the mainstream—this apparently impossible stance achieved by similar principles to those invented by Tesla himself. Somewhere in the lyric "Craft some ritual of industry / To check their progress" lurks the reversed message "You follow me as custard follows a blade's passing." As usual, perceptions differ—other listeners hear the words "Youth only trusts me at my passing" or even "Scoot over my knee, misses, for tonight's pasting." During the fade-out on "Four Hundred Dead in Voting Experiment," Lint (or perhaps the Smile band's Don "Corny" Rensin) can be heard to mumble "Into the minus numbers"—a reference to the time elapsed since Lint's demise? (For more on *Draining* and other Lint music connections see chapter 20.)

For reasons that are still unclear, Doubleday also became briefly convinced in the sixties that Lint was dead, and had planned a series of snazzy reprints of early work until Lint himself stumbled into their offices. In fact, it seems the world was aching for Lint to be out of the picture. It almost got its wish when Hector Gramajo painted a portrait of him in 1970. But the rumor is that if the painting is held at a particular angle it does indeed resemble Lint, puffing into a sadly compliant badger as though into a set of bagpipes. This is supposedly a message urging us to "badger" the publishers to confess that Lint has been replaced by a ringer. The painting is called *Jeff Lint in Smoke*, another hint at accident and obfuscation. Even Lint's "Giraffe" subway poem (beginning "I am not the giraffe you think I am") was seen to imply that he was other than he appeared.

But why would an imposter drop constant hints that he is so? Lint fan Daniel Guyal suggested that Lint's spirit was occasionally possessing his fraudulent replacement, causing the fraud to blunder and give himself away: "Even a cursory glance at the Felix Arkwitch books gives us repeated descriptions of Felix 'unscrambling' from the parallel realms in which he travels concealed. Similarly, the books can be unscrambled." Guyal was an extreme example of obsessive cipher disorder in regard to the Lint myth. His harmless fanzine work in the early eighties (with the photocopied and stapled *Too Pleased to Apologize*) gave way to stalking and marathon decipherment sessions of such an intensity that he became almost blind. In 1992 he pushed his face into the pages of

Fanatique and could not be withdrawn from them. The book had to be surgically cut away, but so much of Guyal's face and skull was missing, it was surmised that he had actually pushed it through into the book's realm—he died within days.

EIGHTEEN

GRAPHIC EQUALIZER: THE CATERER

Against advice ∘ *fogbound motivations* ∘ *Hoston Pete* ∘ *diatribe* ∘
Mouse World ∘ *everything is weird* ∘ *"I won't prevent it"*

"I button myself against advice and leave the house," smirks Jack
Marsden, emerging into primary yellow sunshine. He was a singu-
lar character for Lint who, at a loose end for money in the mid-
seventies, was hired by the fledgling comics company Pearl to
come up with a launch title. Finding fewer compromises here than
in his brief foray into Hollywood in the late sixties, Lint seems to
have taken to the comics scene with the total absorption he gave
his best books. His main contribution to the short-lived Pearl
Comics was the baffling action strip *The Caterer*. Illustrator
Brandon Sienkel worked with Lint in those heady days: "The
Caterer was a strange one—he didn't have any special powers, he

was this blond grinning college kid as far as I could make out. He sometimes pulled a gun. There just didn't seem to be [any rhyme or reason]...the character would fly into a rage about things. But it was strangely hypnotic, I must say. We had fan mail." One such missive, printed in the "Your Yell!" letters page of issue 4, reads: "Dear Caterer, I love your adventures and want to be like you. How can I be the Caterer? I said to my friends your words 'Don't trouble me' and they beat me up on Monday. But I think this is all part of becoming the Caterer." The sign-off at the end reveals the letter to have been from a wide-eyed Martin Amis. All the more disturbing is that he would have been twenty-six at the time.

Much debate has grown up about the meaning of *The Caterer* and any of the nine issues will fetch up to $70 (£2) on eBay. A rare Caterer poster (which portrays Jack Marsden biting the head off a rattlesnake) fetched $100 on RedAuction. Jane Less of Vintage-Globe confirms the specialist interest around the title: "It's a rarity because the company was around for such a short time, the title itself is considered the only true Jeff Lint comic, and finally because it's just so strange." Fans debate its motifs and catch-phrases, and the Caterer's fogbound motivations. "I believe Marsden represents Lint's own creative urge, bursting out at odd moments and killing everybody," says Chris Diana, president of Against Advice: The Caterer Fanclub. "The Caterer is often seen standing at a grave, but we never see the inscription and Marsden has his usual grin on his face. I agree with many readers that this is the grave of Fatty Arbuckle, comedian of the silent era."

Tracing the Caterer's motives is a parlor game for Lint fans. Anyone with a moustache enrages the Caterer, provoking him to "punch that demon from your face and save you from it," an enterprise that often leaves the victim's entire head a bloody mass. He is twice seen to be strangely disarmed by the sight of a spacehopper, standing motionless for fifteen panels (some readers regard the spacehopper as the Caterer's "kryptonite"). His general outlook is one of childish glee at some untold knowledge. "Age is not for acrobats," he smirks at a pompous tailor, before grabbing up a chair and smashing him to the floor. There is speculation that Hoston Pete, a strange piratical character who only visits Jack Marsden in his basement, is a representation of Lint himself. "There is a resemblance," says Sienkel enigmatically. Many readers believe that Hoston Pete is only visible to Marsden and is a schizophrenic "voice" that impels the Caterer to misdeeds. If he is Lint, then this is the author manifesting to direct his characters (shades of Morrison's *Animal Man*). However, in issue 8 the spectral sidekick meets his end when our hero finally notices his moustache.

Several dissertations have been published deconstructing the long, complicated rant in issue 6 about how goats have the skeletal system of chickens (the most incisive being "That's No Scarecrow, It's a Crucifix in a Hat! True Phantoms in *The Caterer*" by Alaine Carraze). The tirade, conducted over five dense pages after Marsden interrupts a school swimming meet, has been interpreted as everything from a critique of Jimmy Carter's then-undisclosed connection to the Trilateral Commission, to a warning about genetic tampering, to homosexual panic (which would jibe with the moustache attacks). Certainly the Caterer's friends are bewildered (or understanding) enough to stand listening to this drivel. But when he tries to leave by riding on an unwilling dog, the cops arrive on the scene and Marsden goes into one of his frenzies. All credit is due to Pearl Comics for depicting the rel-

atively static scene of the diatribe on the cover, rather than the explosive gun battle that follows.

The final (and perhaps least characteristic) issue has the Caterer leaving his small-town setting, visiting a thinly disguised version of Disneyland and simply going berserk. A certain amount of subtlety is lost in this issue and it is still disputed as to whether Pearl Comics was already crashing (and Lint was therefore going out in a blaze) or Lint had gone on some psychological bender that provoked the company's downfall. Sienkel claims that the title was going great guns until the Caterer's "Mouse World" adventure. "The Caterer just rolls up in that strange sedan he was always riding around in, and the minute he gets out he just starts shooting the hell out of everyone. There's hardly even any dialogue. I think at one point he says 'Don't come any closer' or something, but that's it. He's shooting a guy in a duck costume when he says it." This apocalyptic issue caused parents to complain and shocked news vendors to cancel, but it was the threat of legal action from the Disney Company that troubled Pearl executives. It could not be denied that some of the spree victims resembled copyrighted Disney characters (in particular the mouse Satanic Radar Ears) and, with the middling-to-poor sales of other Pearl titles *Fantastic Belt*, *Rocket Trouble* and *The Mauve Enforcer*, Pearl filed for bankruptcy in May 1976.

To kids who read it at the time, it is still a badge of honor. "Other kids were reading *Spiderman* or *Daredevil*, but you knew you were the coolest if you read *The Caterer*. It was like a secret club." It has been said that issue 9 was an influence on *Deathlok the Demolisher*, a title that scared the living shit out of kids during the seventies.

Lint said very little about *The Caterer*, having perhaps been soured on the comic scene by the bland graphic adaptation of *Nose Furnace* in the eighties. "I don't remember much about *The Caterer*," he said in an interview in 1991. "I recall he had issues. Nine, I think. Then they called it all off. God bless him though, why not?"

The Caterer has left a strange cultural legacy. Fans still swap dialogue ("Will you come to my party?" / "I won't prevent it.") and the character rears his sneering head in the likeliest places, as in the various versions of the song *The Caterer/Das Katerer* which litter recent Fall albums. Rumors of movie adaptations come and go (one putatively directed by Tim Burton and starring Brad Pitt), but it's doubtful that the Hollywood system could accommodate it, any more than they could use Lint's own scripts without massive dilution.

As fan club president Chris Diana says, "The Caterer would be sick on today's comics, and on the movies, and on you."

NINETEEN

THE WORLD—IT'S NOT BIG AND IT'S NOT CLEVER

Blast of truth ∘ *drab Tangier* ∘ *psychonauts* ∘ *Elsa Carnesky* ∘
painted Zulu coconuts ∘ *a Hindu cigarette* ∘ *domestic epic anode* ∘
Where are the clams? ∘ *color nodes* ∘ *London* Fanatique ∘
nous sommes assis sur un volcan ∘ *dust devil*

While some have seen the seventies as a time when Lint was spinning his wheels—Plame Tenet claiming in *Starplunge* magazine that Lint's career was "like a pram pushed down stairs"—he was steadily working on the three Arkwitch books, major works that took time to write. This was a departure from his pulp works and he was meanwhile paying his way with scams, *The Caterer*, periodic avoidance of human beings, and very occasional bits of hack journalism. Lint was in fact terrible at "people" journalism, on one occasion asking a chubby guru of the day if he wasn't just an "angelic cushion." At this the holy man snapped "I detect no reverence in your yelling!" Lint had stated the question quite calmly, and concluded that it had been received like a "blast of truth." The article, written for *Rolling Stone*, was titled BLAST OF TRUTH UNSETTLES OLD CODGER, and was never printed. He also interviewed Truman Capote, whom he described as "some sort of wiffling mouse," and had a stint as a sportswriter on the *LA Times*, which he scuppered with his first sentence: "Baseball is: you help a dog, it seems to smile." Still processing the quiet lessons of the Fantastic Lemon, Lint erased his trace from the radar for the bulk of the decade and traveled.

Lint hadn't traveled much. He visited Tangier in 1967 expecting exoticism and intrigue, but rather than people trying to escape, he found only people trying to be noticed. They tried to outshock one another "like trashcan mouths arranged face-to-face—not a very energizing circuit." George Greaves urged him to dress up in drag and Lint, baffled, explained that he had no manuscript to deliver. Bored almost to blindness by the boasting of the dull Rupert Croft-Cooke, Lint kicked him out of a window onto a shop overhang canvas, which split very slowly under Croft-Cooke's weight as he cursed Lint's name. "He was like a slowly submerging ship's captain," said Lint later, "but complaining bitterly." Lint had hoped to find people confident enough to be invisible. Too late he realized they were probably there somewhere, moving around at a deeper focus. But in all, Tangier had deteriorated since the days of Burroughs and Gysin.

Lint was to meet Burroughs again in London in 1971. Visiting his Duke Street flat, Lint tilled through some of Burroughs's fold-in fragments and sat down to do one of his own, folding half a page of published Burroughs into something lying around—to his delight he ended up with a piece of great sense. Lint had hazarded upon one of the strips that Burroughs's text had originally come from, reuniting two parts of some severed Shakespeare. Burroughs, realizing the facts, drawled to a final snap, "You terminal fool, it's supposed to be *gibberish*!"

Lint decided his journeyings should be more exotic, at least involving "leaves and tribal peeking, you know." He started out with a few chancy esoteric perils in the Colombian jungle. Lint recorded his observations in letters to Rouch. "Jungle adventure tends to inconvenience monkeys—they are stared at, cooed over, and shot. No wonder they shriek when observed." Not that anyone really needed a reason. Lint had elected to try yage, a drug brewed up for him by the *brujo* Magal Seam near Puerto Limon. There was another psychonaut there at the same time, a twenty-seven-year-old artist named Elsa Carnesky. She told Lint she had become blocked when attempting to portray "an Anglican bishop with a terrified expression," and decided to solve the problem by locating an Anglican bishop and very observantly rushing at him with a raised dagger. The ensuing trouble left her disillusioned with the art establishment and she had set out on a mission to locate a totally new and unseen color. She discovered that such colors were always present but that human consciousness screened them out because they did not fit existing definitions. Lint was reminded of his own alien-color-invasion tale "Lipstick & Shells" and his hunting for nameless colors as a child. He and Carnesky drank the brew and looked out at the tatty jungle.

A roulette sea spiraled to Lint's center, illuminating the cranium in curious flashes, and then a narcotic concussion nearly blew the eyes out of his head. He wrote of the experience: "Drowsy empires flutter in some elemental distance, I chase over colors and proportion to observe the hazardous bliss of canyons, the glowing yards of platform factories, black whales passing over dead tops of towers, pullulating system creatures, the purple darkness changing in tiers, anatomy adhering to its walls." He watched comparative chances streaming like waterfalls inside a phenomenal landscape.

Somewhere in all this Lint turned to see that Elsa Carnesky was striding a cinematic hero-world, the toughest cowgirl gunslinger in the echoey west, her theme tune reminding him of her amazing identity. An intensity of painted desert scrolled past her, sheriff stars falling from the sky. He was stunned by this sacred Technicolor heart of Elsa and his experience of her would be forever affected by the vision.

Looking down to observe red and blond blood cells teeming through his arm, he noticed that letters were falling on dirt to twitch like worms and shrivel to nothing. In researching maverick substances in text-DNA, Lint had nipped at the heels of a process he called tagging, in which atoms and molecules could be labeled with words and concepts and allowed to weave texts by natural processes. The main problem was getting to a state where the atomic was visible and the observer was in a fit state to creatively record those observations—Lint briefly thought he had found a way, and returned to the rotting and fertile jungle "with the scent of heaven still on my hands." The old *brujo* scrutinized Lint and said he had seen volcanic sludge feeding toward him, each little light in it pulsing like a code.

Carnesky told Lint she had spent the whole trip talking to a spider with an abdomen the size of a spacehopper.

But for Lint the experience wasn't over. The next day he walked out to greet an X-ray, the crisp cataclysm of the morning, heaven's unasked-for confessions scalding his brain. Nature was the blue-eyed unkindness of children, a cold necessary blade. "What we will find is the hair of our soul, an earthy force acting upon itself." Raw value was spreading surflike, the endless accident of the universe including the etheric angst of those become conscious of it. "The flavor of obliteration wasn't so bad," he wrote later. "A bit like boiled sprouts." Lint's zebra heart broke at angles to the stripes.

Lint and Elsa traveled on together and enjoyed Mexico's Day of the Dead celebrations, "a vaudevillian skull amid prophecy and pastries." But it was amid the sugar heads and fortune music of New Orleans's Mardi Gras, snapshot flowers leaving stains on his eye, that Lint realized he was in love with Elsa. "She had one of those smiles that went upside down, using all the muscles," said Lint. "It worked her whole face. She wasn't afraid to crack her mask." Lint tried to impress her by taking part in a ritual test of endurance. "The cake was difficult to eat, being made of mashed blindfolds. But by god I made a go of it."

There followed more than a year of world travel with Carnesky. Lint filtered all through his hauntbones or, as Lord Pin put it, "mastered the Thousand Sights and came out saying blimey."

Describing a still stick insect: "A moment on the green leaf, sham twigs."

Restaurants: "Short wine glass? Curse their game."

London: "A mistake built to last a thousand years."

Border guards: "tend to be the sort of men who like being observed."

The Rainforest: "These pythons are always on the go."

Their trip to India, a land "teeming with deities," included a visit to a cavern lined with earlobes. "The locals have told us this cave is where humanity's earlobes wind up after death, and I'm inclined to believe them. Why would they lie about something so unimportant?"

A local swami told Lint "Electricity can't be shocked—neither can one who is enlightened." To which Lint made a graceless allusion to Thomas Merton and complained about the fixtures in the local hostels. "Tropical plugs are a different color," he recorded elsewhere. Lint wrote of foyer world, of the check-in desk with its "lion telephone like a golden bottle."

As if repeatedly encountering *Jelly Result*'s town of Eterani, Lint would conclude from his travels that "All cities are designed for the same scenarios."

"Even my luggage is aching," Lint wrote to Alan Rouch, and concluded that he was "too old for rotted sleeping bags and licking the mountain."

He and Elsa were married in Oaxaca in 1975 and lived there awhile, Elsa painting landscapes under "the sun, an epic anode," and Lint writing to Rouch that "they have a very large daytime over here." "To do nothing isn't inherently bad," he told poet Sue Diebold. "It depends what you're doing nothing about."

Lint told Rouch these were "Happy days. Distorted rats are pulled from melons. Falling into the undergrowth presents no real difficulties. What is commonly called money is really a series of photographic snapshots of the death process. Come join us, Alan."

Rouch visited and found a mild domestic scene, both Lint and Carnesky working productively in the adobe house. Lint went on about how every location opens up into every other location (something he had already described in the first Arkwitch book). During Rouch's stay he witnessed the beginning of the fan phenomenon that would grow around Lint, when a young reader showed up on the doorstep with books to sign and arcane questions. Presumably in reference to the *Draining* album, the nervous kid wanted to know how an anteater knows its responsibilities. Perhaps feeling obliged to profundity, Lint thought a little while. "In the atoms of things," he said, "are details like decrees. The intent of the creator is stored in the creation. That's why wood sounds certain and metal merely inflexible." Lint was now something of a recluse and described the mild conversation as a "violent novelty." His only advice to young writers was "ignoring newts," something that surely went without saying.

Another time he told a bothersome fan to "go across town and hassle Castaneda." The fan said he didn't believe anything Lint said. Lint claimed that he was not used to having his words doubted, a quip that provoked caustic laughter from his young wife.

Working on *Fanatique*, Lint enjoyed describing the textured oasis around him, the white-noise ethanol sky, hot tin chassis in weeds, and the crinkled feeling of tree. "A spider like a shiny bead, eyelashes growing from the side of a wall, a pressing heat before thunder relieves the sky."

One morning Elsa snapped at him "You're selfish" and Lint, thinking she'd said "Your shellfish," sat waiting for her to present him with some sort of seafood platter. After ten silent, staring minutes he demanded "Well? Where are the clams?" and Elsa went into the bedroom to pack her stuff. Lint was baffled and bereft after the breakup and his writing routine, which he usually described as "interlocking structures of towering fire," suffered. When he did write, birds "rummaged through the air" instead of being described properly.

Lint was experimenting with "the beading of creativity in an almost-vacuum," by which color denied gathers to a node or very disparate nodes—in this case, to Lint himself—where it is utilized and appreciated. London seemed the perfect venue, but he mistimed his arrival in Britain—the vacuum he expected would not hit for another few years. As it was he found a major color node already blushing out in the form of punk, a rare outbreak of honesty in a covertly brutal nation. "The Japanese will hand you a business card with both hands," Lint wrote, "the British will propel you under a train the same way." But during his sojourn in London in 1976–77 he would form links with the punk and nascent industrial scene, raising his profile further among the young. By now looking like a grinning bone ghost of a hawk and striding the streets in a white leather coat (Malcolm McLaren called him "a living knife"), he found he could scare the shit out of anyone looking for trouble just by creasing his ageing face.

Lint continued to experiment. Inspired by Gex's poem about events in Chile in 1974, "Santiago," in which a firsthand description of the U.S.-backed massacre of 9/11 was simply divided up into lines, Lint did a similar thing with Kissinger's green light to Suharto's genocide in East Timor:

> the use of U.S.-made arms
> could create problems
> our risks of being found out
> our efficiency is cut
> our main concern is that whatever you do
> does not create a climate
> that discourages investment

we will do our best to keep everyone quiet
until the president returns home

He tried imposing Perecian constraints on his writing and many code-derived passages turn up in *Fanatique*, such as the Oulipo ("o" in every word) chapter "Blood Orange Apocalypse."

"Lord only knows how Ollie overruled our orthodox proposals."
"Oh, Ollie's not so honest."
"How so?"
"Too old. Poorly codgers often obstruct out of outright orneriness."

He also worked with SOA code, by which each word must begin alternately with the first and last letters of those in the text of U.S. torture manuals. Thus the CIA's *KUBARK Counterintelligence Interrogation Manual*:

The following are the principal coercive techniques of interrogation: arrest, detention, deprivation of sensory stimuli through solitary confinement or similar methods, threats and fear, debility, pain, heightened suggestibility and hypnosis, narcosis, and induced regression.

is raw source for the following text (from chapter 7 of *Fanatique*):

To go about energized, put everyone to flight immediately through drawling nonsense or yelling something heretical. Soon the old rules may seem absolutely random. Decisions needn't hold you. A slave's negative decision is noble.

But these and other experiments, including a sojourn in Paris, couldn't distract from Lint's loneliness after Elsa's departure. He traveled to visit her in Elora, Canada. But upon arrival he peered in through the window of her huge barn studio to find it filled with dozens of paintings portraying him as the Devil incarnate, biting the head off a little lamb. He went away again bereft, and visited Rouch in LA.

Rouch was going from strength to strength in TV land, with preproduction starting on his crime series *Everywhere We Go, People Die* (later retitled *Hart to Hart*). He suggested that Lint throw a few ideas at the studio. "Chuck a load of trash directly at their faces and see what sticks behind their shades," said Rouch. "And for God's sake don't laugh."

Lint went to see ABC exec Lyndon Eagleburger and proposed a TV movie about an air pilot who was incredibly skilled, but who screamed the entire time he was off the ground. "He isn't even scared," Lint explained. "It's just a medical reaction. After the war he gets work as a commercial pilot and his shrieked captain announcements instill stark panic and terror in the passengers, even when he's commenting on the beautiful weather and perfect adherence to the timetable." Finally he becomes a hero when a hijacker, entering the cockpit to find the captain screaming like a bastard as he grips the wheel, concludes that the plane is going down and faints like a cartoon wife.

"I think it's a crappy idea," Eagleburger told him and Lint threw himself across the desk, strangling Eagleburger with one hand and stealing an ashtray with the other. Lint was thrown out of the studio building with Eagleburger's final advice ringing in his ears: "Irrespective of you trying to strangle me, I still think it's a crappy idea."

Lint sold the ashtray for almost nothing, but felt satisfied by what he'd learned: "There's a fine line between real entertainment and a tightrope walker."

It was not until the eighties and the horrors of *Nose Furnace* and *Caterer the Movie* that Lint would deal with Hollywood again.

TWENTY

SWAYING FAST IS ROCKING

Lint rock ○ The Energy Draining Church Bazaar ○ *flies* ○ *trun* ○
strange incidents ○ *a policy of terrorizing* ○ *bloat* ○ *cable cheese* ○ *Unsmile* ○
The Prophecies ○ *on reading new books* ○ *explorers are never suspicious*

"Music can be lengthy, some kinds get the soul," Lint told *Zig Zag* magazine in 1969. Lint's claim to musical fame at the time was an album of pellucid ravings, *The Energy Draining Church Bazaar,* recorded with the Unofficial Smile Group. Lint seemed to blunder effortlessly into such projects, his young fanbase seeing in him an icon of far-outness. From the late sixties onward he was regularly adopted by rock movements and pasted into their agenda, whether in The Fall's "Caterer" tracks or in the raucous crowd of a bar in Dylan's *Renaldo and Clara,* laughing as Ruth Tyrangiel urges Dylan to "bare yourself like the cross." The Crystal City Martyrs (named after motor fatalities among Lint wedgers) made several Lint references in their eponymous first album, such as the graveyard lion in "Gong Over Crib: That's Discipline."

In the case of *Draining*, the Smile band was on the verge of splitting when Lint rolled up with a dumb song about flies:

> One half of the truth is that
> The eye loves a coffin

"It creeped me out a bit," says Don "Corny" Rensin in his autobiography *Crooked Smile*. "And he kept saying that 'flies can be awfully dismissive.' But two of the others had heard of him, and it was those times, and we got together." Gabriel Hutton and "Judge" Pete Fox had read Lint and were flattered that he had written a song for them. "Foxy even tried to impress Lint by saying something like 'brocade doesn't last long in the North Sea,' but Lint just stared at him."

Lint, whom Rensin described as "a scary, freakishly strong old man," began a collaboration with the fragile group, writing an albumful of songs that he reworked as rehearsals progressed. He took to showing up at the Mission Hills rehearsal house to oversee progress. "One time he turned up in some sort of carpet coat," says Rensin, "smacking snow out of it like Dr. Zhivago. We looked outside and it was perfectly sunny."

Lint's presence began to permeate the project, his ideas for new sounds sparking the others to invention. "He'd say. 'I want a sound like a hot moon bursting like a bubble and dropping atom-size hens in the sea' or something—in fact *exactly* that, and that's the sound we came up with for 'Memory X-Ray Hammer.'" Fox created the sound by hitting a melon with a frypan while letting out a sort of keening wail. The recorded sound was then slowed right down and thrown away, along with the rest of the song.

The "pragment" had been the beginning of Lint's habit of inventing words. By now he was having stories rejected for his use of words like *spile* (bitterness on a wet, yellow-colored day), *spagran* (gangly stranger with probable unhealthy habits), and *trun* (stubborn outthrust of chin upon almost facing the truth). One unused story began, "Walking out, I felt a pang of spile" and goes on to describe a spagran who, upon being observed, gives it a "bit of trun." The occupants of 10619 Sepulveda Boulevard began to converse in similar terms, visitors finding the place like a tar pit from which almost anything could emerge. The previously accomplished Hutton found he had become inept and had to relearn his playing as though the guitar were an alien object. "Lint seemed to want to rewrite us," says Hutton today. Lint would term their rehearsals "a stiff daily godlet tasting of tetanus" and persistently addressed drummer David Owen as "Comrade Plunge." Owen remembers a groupie injecting "brimstone endorphine" directly into her forehead and saying in a monotone, "Spiders manage without us and wires don't care. An argument against." The statement shows up in "DNA Interruption Charm," a song that on the album segues with confounding ease into the band's celebration of the joys of the country, "Mesmerized by Midges."

It seems that the scariness many attributed to the older Lint was beginning to manifest at around this time, along with the inexplicable visual quirks that fans were to witness in later years. Many strange incidents have been recounted by those who have availed themselves of the un-signposted public right-of-way through Lint's head. Daniel Guyal of the Lint fanzine *Too Pleased to Apologize* told of Lint sitting at his window and very slowly becoming a piled construction of glass shells. Approaching these finally, Guyal found that the objects were so brittle and airy that they disintegrated at his touch, blowing away like the lightest of skin flakes. In the hysterical enclave of the Sepulveda house, Lint's creative strangeness was sending everyone into weird coping postures. Fox wrote at the time: "Waking in the morning's like looking out a plane window and seeing the wing's on fire." Their predicament seemed to go beyond psychodrama. Lint set rules for times when group members could leave the house, but these times did not exist on any actual clock—Lint called it Newt Horology. Like clipper sailors ready to quit and retire to dry land, the band now found their ship commandeered by an insanely unpredictable pirate. Lint terrorized them. "He would bring us instruments I'd never seen before, like the one that was a triangular shadow. He told me to touch the edges and it had pulsing filaments there, like the legs of a millipede. He set it down on the floor and it flowed steadily away into a corner. I never went near that shadowy corner again. And then there was Damage Night."

Rensin's account of "Damage Night" is that when the group was utterly asleep at four A.M., Lint entered in a blast of light, dressed as the Devil and screaming something about blood. "He was wearing a really orange fright wig and his eyes were weird, like they'd been peeled. The antlers on him were just massive, scraping across the ceiling."

"He had some sort of portable kleig light set up behind him, I think," says Hutton, "and a photographer's lamp in his hand, uplighting his face so the shadows were tearing around all over the joint. And the *screaming* ... "

Fox recalls: "His mouth opened way further than it should, like a black bag, and the screaming of several women came out of it." [16]

Owen disagrees. "His mouth was pursed and as small as an eyelid. But his body was rolling like a huge ball, and parts of his arms were far away from his body—like an octopus."

"He was a cloud of flies with a face in the middle," Fox states simply. "I can't explain it, but that's what entered the room that night."

Owen again: "There were limbs angle-poised off it like little construction cranes with white gloves on the end, all dripping soup."

"I saw W. C. Fields come in and say we were all done for," says Hutton.

"He never said that thing about 'the blood in thee harms the gods,'" Fox states. "He was shouting this 'death to empty patience' stuff, and repeated a part that went 'Tie a clown to a chair as a tornado approaches. Feel the joy and fear battling within you? *That*'s what it's like to create.'"

"He told us there was something wrong with his bones, and that we had to wrap them," Rensin recalls.

"I thought he said something about the Confederates," says Owen.

"He just wouldn't stop screaming," says Fox.

Hutton thinks Lint was wearing a magic "johnny-hat."

Whatever the outrages perpetrated upon the Unofficial Smile Group, it resulted in the "sonic failure hurricane" that was *The Energy Draining Church Bazaar*. The track list is:

SIDE 1

1. Hydrogen Sheriff

2. Roses Own That Town

3. The Pangolin and the Anteater Have a Fight

4. Pocket Man Schedule

5. Ignore Tesla

6. The Varnished Biology of Seafish

7. Four Hundred Dead in Voting Experiment

8. You Are Early

SIDE 2

1. DNA Interruption Charm

2. Mesmerized by Midges

3. Through the Keyhole I Saw the Funeral of a Duck

4. Would You Mind Not Doing That?

5. Roses Own That Town (reprise)

6. The Number Nineteen Is Made of Wax

7. The Delaware Christ

8. Dead or Not, He Was Wearing Shades

The album was recorded under what Fox called "trying conditions," with Lint draping himself over the cymbals to create a more "organic" sound and Hutton weeping into his bass. They are angular, sidelong songs with cascading lyrics and oblique correspondences all over. "Pocket Man Schedule" zigzags like a policy, Rensin a dry voice blowing around and through fossilized instruments. "The cello had a joystick," says Rensin today. "Roses Own That Town" is a song that swells slowly like a red balloon, slow and gluey bongos loping against a sitar shimmer like gold Argo sails.

The song becomes a skittish conjuration. "Pressure to conform ejects the soap," yelps Rensin. In "You Are Early" several melodies overlap amid out-of-sync screaming about "bargains" from the group as Rensin's voice distorts into the guitar mix and emerges the other end as, yes, Lint's voice, dwindling into the fade before we can tell whether the writer can sing.

In the manner of the day, listeners tried to decode the lyrics—Lint learned that the simple act of sticking his words on an album sleeve would get people to scrutinize them more closely than on the pages of a book. "Pocket Man Schedule" was fairly straightforward:

> Most establishments
> are the false ardently maintained
> stronger than us through scaffolding
> repetition-trained

But things get more open to florid interpretation with the pleased hyena character in the final track and the sinister egg of "The Number Nineteen Is Made of Wax," "liquid gears swelling in the embryo." This latter track halts abruptly as Lint breaks in bellowing "In music the interval is not an embellishment god dammit, I *told* you that didn't I?"

There are theories (see the Smile Group chapter in Kate Senser's *Holy Flame of Surprise*) that the entire album is about heroic-level drug ingestion and the resultant neon lethargy. Lint, whose head was a firestormed funfair at the best of times, seems rarely to have indulged. His yage experiment was in the context of shamanic practice, as were the reported occasions of his "stepping out of existence" in the midst of conversation. The charismatic psychopath John Dyche claimed to have heard voices in "Would You Mind Not Doing That?" ordering him to carve a totem pole out of Peter Fonda, a task it is uncertain he achieved.

Many listeners can't help feeling a literary bloat after the *Draining* ordeal. Things weren't helped at the time by Lint's gnomic pronouncements to the music press, where his abnormal and creepy suppositions were becoming notorious. He told *Melody Maker* he was "cheese on a cable. I will stay. Or will I?" Chaim Skipjack of *Floozie* zine asked for follow-up info on the cable cheese.

LINT: Necessary for my answer is a perfectly brutal confession, a sort of barrelling at the facts like a snorter.
SKIPJACK: Well I can't help you there. What are you going to do now?
LINT: Sunbathe so long I get a palm tree through my belly.

In 1970 he told Richard Front of the *Los Angeles Free Press*: "The universe is full of unbelievable bastards. Your name has been mentioned in this connection." Front launched himself across the table and strangled Lint, whose pop-eyed and wild-haired visage at that instant was photographed for the issue's cover.

The press were divided on the album's merits, their assessments ranging from "a quicksilver transaction of nameless magic" through "it leads us aside and bites us suddenly, bringing the party to a shocked halt" to "you may as well put an omelet on the turntable." Today Rensin says there were problems connected with "the business side of things" and the fact that this side of things "did not exist." Hutton claims the album was the result of a misunderstanding. The Smile band took a two-year period of recuperation and recovery before their first attempt at commercial stadium rock, *Prod Me*. After two more bland "progressive" albums as Unsmile (*Terra Pocus* and *Open the Goddamn Door*), they split amid an incoherent tangle of grudges.

Lint, meanwhile, continued to collide, now and again, with the music industry. During his residence in London he encountered the nascent industrial scene and met up with fans Spurtwife, whose track "Ossuary TV" referred to images in the then-obscure *Prepare to Learn*. U.S. punk band Zombie Supply Teacher and UK pub rockers Fucking Bender both wrote songs about Arkwitch, and the ethereal Cocteau Twins-alikes Nectargirl Climbs On produced a "sound track" to the Arkwitch trilogy with the album *Amateur Saints Blunder Through Visions and Fear of Injury*. Lint's 1991 CD with Stan Esswell (guitarist with Corposant) in which he reads from *Easy Prophecy* material (*The Prophecies*) is now a collector's item, and the movement has continued apace since Lint's death, with Carlotta Flame and the industrial subsonic outfit Perfect Interruption referencing *Clowns and Locusts* and *The Stupid Conversation*.

Lint equated the freedom of musical experimentation with travel to exotic climes. "Explorers are never suspicious, are they?"

In 1970 an interview with Lint appeared in *IT* and Lint spoke about the connection that occurs between two disparate objects "via the billion billion intervening forms that the two objects are not—the trip between those two objects, even if they're just a spoon and a salt shaker here on this table, really is a trip." The same was true of two ideas—if Lint was presented with a choice between two philosophies, he would see the billion billion other philosophies between those two, "and then those extended outside that created line, and in all other directions. In other words, there are options."

TWENTY-ONE

NOSE FURNACE AND OTHER DEATHS

Suction eel ∘ *satan filters* ∘ *factoids* ∘ *The Insufferable Banyolar* ∘
Arkwitch the Movie ∘ *Aquadog* ∘ Platypus Payback ∘
where is Durutti? ∘ The Caterer *in limbo*

In Lint's 1958 book *Nose Furnace* a new devil gives hell a makeover, sweetening the brimstone with marzipan and generally missing the point. The novel is narrated by a sort of suction eel living near a sulfur chimney, making merry in the gas. For some reason this was the first of Lint's books to be seriously considered for a movie. Lint was fine with it. "It's best that my books were used for these things—if I'd written and developed stuff especially for the screen, the studios would have intercepted my ideas before they got too good."

Contained too long, a coiled spring may lose its stored potential. Lint had got to know the publishing industry the way

people ease into winter, but for a writer the movie system was a
world of barred studios and gratitude only confessed in deepest
nightshade. So he never took it too seriously. Lint had become
quite a raconteur, but purely on his terms, as at a gathering for
Tony Curtis's birthday at which he stood and described a process
of cutting slivers of devil to place over a camera lens—these
"satan filters" were impossible to market, he claimed, because
they disclosed the evil of whoever was being filmed as a scrambling acidic corrosion. He knew, because he had tested it on
Benny Hill. This rambling diatribe, nested as it was among the
other guests' tributes to Curtis, got him thrown out and he rolled
down a verge into Mulholland Drive. "Even their cruelty was
half-baked and anemic," wrote Lint. "They didn't seem capable
of organizing anything."

Lint deplored the impersonal sterility of the 1980s. "Everyone
moves so fast. Stop to say something and you lose your friends."
He was finishing the last Arkwitch book and planning several
other works including the *Easy Prophecy* series. "At that time,"
Lint later recalled, "my thoughts fell on me like bits of ceiling. And
all the books were long-term."

The media adaptations and apparent lack of new raw product
led Gore Vidal to say of Lint, "He was once a genius—he's now a
born-again mediocrity." Lint fans have asserted that he would
never have conceded to such projects as *Into the Nose Furnace*, but
he was a pragmatic fellow and did a fair bit of hack work at times
of low funds ("Money disappears like ice," he wrote, "even when
it's freezing.") These jobs tended to bear the "mark of Lint," however. *The Caterer* comic, after all, was a work for hire—so was his
rejected *Star Trek* episode. For a few months in the early eighties

he wrote jokes and "factoids" for candy wrappers, his offerings including "The stinkbug is a force for good," "Yuri Gagarin screamed upon reentry," and "I'm not scared of you." He also accepted a commission to produce a subway poem which, he was directed, had to be about "The Giraffe." The poem rushed beneath New York giving everyone the heebie-jeebies:

> *I am not the giraffe you think I am*
> *I do not run as if in slow motion*
> *I scream like an anvil-eared skull*
> *And blast at your window like lightning*

This was after all the man who said "When the abyss gazes into you, bill it."

With his interest in magic Lint followed the activities of the Insufferable Banyolar, an audience-resenting stage illusionist who saw fit to hide his disgusted sneer in a lion's mouth. The inevitable accident that ended his earthly career inspired Lint to propose an appalling kids' toy based on the incident. Lint was so persistent that one company paid him a "kill fee" to bugger off.[17]

At another time Lint got the idea for a food product consisting of shaped pieces of "boneless and chinless" fish, which Lint wanted to market as "Chicken of Heaven." He told Alan Rouch that he thought it might be possible sell the idea to a food company and then "disappear" as if he had never existed. Rouch suggested that the product could be marketed with the tagline "A test of faith."

Another supposed cash cow was "Spatial Awareness Snot," a magnetized resin that was supposed to give the user a birdlike perception of direction and geophysical positioning. In fact it was just some sandwich jelly and any additional instincts it bestowed upon insertion into the human nose was purely the result of resentment and cheated rage.

Lint also pitched an alternate-universe *Spiderman* strand to Marvel: "What if Spiderman knew he was a Waste of Space?"

But many fans have never believed that Lint allowed the frozen decade to waste his time, and this more than anything has led to rumors of undiscovered masterpieces. It is known that he trained a hundred octopi to flash particular messages along their flanks and then released them back into the wild, hoping that they might combine and recombine to create different stories. He was also said to have used a sea horse as a party blower.

By the time the movie of *Nose Furnace* fell through, it had attracted the attention of Wallent Comics, who set upon a disastrous adaptation of their own. Their take on the story was that Santa Claus is put in charge of Hades, in response to which Lucifer sends a bounty hunter to kill him. Bloated and bland, the *Nose Furnace* graphic novel is a product to rival Disney and its heart-smart dollars.

Though his devotees perpetuated the myth that he was the result of an ovum fertilized by a comma, Lint kept up regular contact with his mother, who was now living in Florida. She was never one to slow down—indeed she seems to have gained a new lease on life since the death of her own parents. In recent years her health had not been good, however, and when Lint went to see her in 1981 she was clearly ailing. Liver cancer had been diagnosed. A few months later she suffered her second stroke in two years. Pulmonary complications meant that she had to slow down. It was a surprise to everyone when, at a stunt-bike performance by Jetkid Eezie at Seaworld, she volunteered to ride pillion behind the daredevil during a jump over a pool of angry tiger sharks. A misaligned springboard caused the jet bike to hit the wall of the fire tunnel and rebound into the shark tank—the sharks were mechanical but the bike's jet ignited their gas feeds, causing an explosion. Carol Lint and Jetkid Eezie were killed.

At the funeral Lint spoke of how Carol was constantly dodging death, such as the time she went to get in her car and heard the hissing of the tire going down, then called a mechanic only to have him point out that the source of the hissing was an eleven-foot alligator waiting under the vehicle. "Oblivion doesn't always wait till after dinner," Lint concluded. "If the period of trial is subtracted from our eternal reward, Mother did well to die at such velocity." The priest waited until the other mourners had dispersed before kicking him in the stomach.

"Perhaps putting a byline to truth is as pointless as painting a torpedo," Lint wrote in his journal, feeling futile.

The one project that raised its head with regularity in Hollywood was the possibility of a movie based around Felix Arkwitch, star of *The Stupid Conversation*, *Fanatique*, and later *The Phosphorus Tarot of Matchbooks* (the last outlined in manuscript at this time). The supposed bidding war between Mickey Rourke and a young Tom Cruise to play *The Caterer*'s Jack Marsden caused Lint's stock to rise in Hollywood and Warner Bros. optioned the Arkwitch series, setting a committee to work on a script which would roll the books into one. While Lint said that *The Stupid Conversation* was "a surrender to the bathysphere part of the human mind," the movie version seems to have been written with the part of the mind that controls the knee. "I wouldn't dream of interfering with Greg Churilov's screenplay," wrote Lint in a message to Warners. "After all, it is shit."

In the proposed movie *Stargun Warrior*, Arkwitch was recast as a freewheeling astronaut who lives in a space station outfitted with a whirlpool bath. But Earth is threatened when a group of people from its own nuclear-blasted future travel back in time to invade and forcibly colonize the present. A clock in the lower left corner of their eyesight tells them their remaining life span. Any Lint-written scenario would have the invaders discover what a boring wasteland eighties Earth is and returning to their deadly future, but in the movie the appalling cold of things is utterly ignored. Arkwitch[18] merely destroys the invaders with some sort of makeshift rocket. It was a crappy rewrite to rival Schwarzenegger's "The human should win against the vampires" demand re *I Am Legend*.

The studio decided to add Aquadog, a bouncy purple bastard that audiences are supposed to find lovable as it knocks important stuff off the shelves. The other characters are always having to go back to rescue it from villainous aliens, and Lint sent a memo to the studio that included these remarks:

"Regarding Aquadog, I think it would be more realistic and less irritating for the crew to leave him behind on the Death Planet, or hunt him down and kill him aboardship before they arrive there. Those laser crossbows are perfect for it and the onscreen time could be filled with close-ups of Cindy Morgan's ass."

Warners accepted no more messages or calls from Lint and he was cut off from the project. The *Arkwitch* movie, in fact, was never made and the never-released Aquadog merchandise fetches large sums on eBay today. The figures are designed to jitter and jump hyperactively while spouting catchphrases like "Porthole? I thought it was a spin dryer" and "Well, it got a reaction!" Many collectors buy the toys purely to set them alight and watch them twitch for the last time.

Once again at Alan Rouch's urging, Lint proposed a pilot for a TV show: *Platypus Payback*. In the show three members of the public must go to dinner with an animatronic platypus that bellows arcane obscenities in the voice of a sheep while shooting flames from its eyes and spewing blue slime over everyone. It's not surprising the show wasn't picked up, this being almost two decades before the heyday of reality TV.

As for the Rourke/Cruise project, the execs invited Lint to the studio so that they could ignore him in person, but he showed up wearing some sort of Styrofoam bathysphere held up by braces. When they became annoyed at having to acknowledge this faux pas, he started kicking them with the end of his legs. "Muted by attention," he claimed later, referring perhaps to the entire Hollywood experience, "I couldn't think."

Caul Pin, the eccentric false Lord who once ran down a conference table kicking everyone seated there, has informed opinions on Lint's performance: "The mere fact that Lint was kicking them all at the same time was as good as proof that their faults were related. As he himself wrote, 'Paradox results from artificial boundaries.'"

This was also the time of Lint's attendance at the LA Sci-Fi Convention and his strange collapse during a Q and A session. At the emergency ward he was discovered to have a wristband stating that he was "Batman Intolerant."

Caterer the Movie is in turnaround limbo to this day.

Soon after the publication of *The Phosphorus Tarot of Match-books* Lint got the hell out of LA and rarely looked back at it from Taos, New Mexico. "Forgive California," he wrote. "A bit of land more sinned against than sinning."

TWENTY-TWO

ARKWITCH

Thousand Mile Gun ∘ *the slug correspondence* ∘ *mind-mapping* ∘
satire as sacrament ∘ *sheer visual quantity evokes the magical*
resonance of the tribal horde ∘ *behind the text*

Incredible, mind-bending scenes of the spirit form Felix navigating septic vertices and unscrambling amid tricky standoffs are two-a-penny in the Arkwitch books, which are regarded, along with *Jelly Result* and *Clowns and Locusts*, as Lint at his dismissive best. An atomic equation in skin, Arkwitch samples one heaven a week while phasing through blast walls and wrecking everything. Thorough detection-evasion technology means that oppression changes his body from instant to instant. He can appear as a coppersmith ruining a porpoise talisman, a grimly staring Secoya Indian, or a mere ornamental oaf. His adventures are punctuated with glimpses of a sort of angel depot, arcane scenes of Arkwitch consulting with Acres (a Victorian robot with a face like a giant postage stamp), and the sheer primal terror unleashed when he fires his Thousand Mile Gun (only once in each book), as in *Fanatique* when he punishes humanity for treating certain species as if they were the amateur parts of nature.

The Stupid Conversation kicked off the series. Knowing that Tom Delay will be instrumental in the destruction of the world, Arkwitch traps him and a colleague in an etheric syntax loop, whereby they talk bullshit endlessly and cannot leave the house. But Arkwitch himself becomes trapped with them and must plot his escape without their detection in a classic closed-loop crime scenario:

> FELIX: I suppose if you must amuse yourself you could put some underpants on that hen over there and watch it walking about. Don't let it get in the sink.
>
> DELAY: Wow, thanks, Mr. Arkwitch.
>
> FELIX: I mean it. Don't let it get in the sink, all right? And don't do anything stupid like . . . dressing up as a woman or something.
>
> DELAY: Why would I do that?
>
> FELIX: Because the safety of the world depends on it.

"This *Conversation* is *Stupid* all right," declared Babs Mueller of the *Los Angeles Times*. "Just once I'd like to see Lint try harder than a grape. Just once. He isn't even looking at what he's typing anymore."

But Felix Arkwitch was a hit with the readers. He was a hero they could relate to because he flirted with cattle and wore failure like a badge of validation. Sometimes Arkwitch decides his day should be spent "kerning" the air around his head, which involves his doing strange swirling hand motions while chiding the atmosphere with the words "Now now, none of that!"

Arkwitch's clothing is always detailed in full, even when he is not wearing it—thus every day the entire content of his wardrobe is listed, with only occasional additions altering the otherwise identically repeated paragraphs. Sean Eaglestone of the London *Times* described these passages as "the worst kind of appalling self-indulgence, deadly to the soul—I'm afraid I used torn pages from *The Stupid Conversation* to flick a fairly small slug off the path. And it came back."

Lint wrote to Eaglestone saying he suspected him of merely stamping on the snail and kicking it away like the coward he probably was. "Stare at yourself in the mirror long enough, your face disappears," wrote Lint. "And good riddance."

Lint was reportedly shouting with laughter as he wrote the letter, but Eaglestone seems to have taken umbrage and his response was printed on the letters page next to Lint's missive. Claiming that the only other Lint book he had seen was the DAW reprint of *Jelly Result*, Eaglestone described that work as a contributing factor to his failing health, that it reminded him of a small useless hammer carved out of a potato, and that a yellow stain was vibrating in the air before his eyes. Lint wrote back recommending an exercise suspiciously similar to Arkwitch "airkerning," at which Eaglestone replied two days later that he was famished, all color had "fled the garden," and everything was now just falling away from him like gray feathers. Eaglestone's dismal obituary appeared in the following issue. In his essay "Not Fit for the Barn," Dan Mitrione has opined that the entire correspondence was a setup and that Eaglestone was in fact Lint's friend "Lord" Caul Pin, who was back in England at the time and bursting with life and energy.

Fanatique begins with an episode in which a group of politicians holed up in an Arctic station try to discover which one of them is actually a human being in disguise. "No smartass New York lawyer can stop me doing *this*!" shouts Ollie Seacoal, a zany welder with connections. His violent solution to his guests' dilemma leaves the pole drenched in gore. But ice has a memory and Arkwitch, carrying out a mellow inspection in some kind of Arcadian drug mill, is alerted to an equally malign presence approaching humanity. His solution involves his traveling back in time to ride through portions of history with irony generators mounted on donkey carts. The book's best moments are in the firefly feedback of time-pain and the cinematic dazzle as Felix walks through the stereo avarice of the city. Through his silver eyes, flesh and commotion are the mere paraphernalia of the soul.

Lint was by now getting a rep as a fearsome fella and that interpersonal scariness manifested in the writing of *Fanatique*, which contains some of the creepiest set pieces of any Lint book. A kid tries to sleep as he watches a developing water stain on the ceiling that resembles a face—the attic is of course filled with a massive child's head the size of a whale, and when the eyes slip open the childhead asks in a child's voice to be fed on "new blood." Elsewhere, a husband turns out to be not a living creature but a deception of anatomical junk and gutting mined from dolls. A strange cinema projects the silent decay process of a celebrity in real time for select patrons. A hospital customer returns screaming, night whistles plugged in his eyes—other death candidates are not so lucky.

Lint's mid-seventies wedge experiments had got him to

thinking about mind-map programming and he finally put this to work in *The Phosphorus Tarot of Matchbooks* (published in 1988). In the book he establishes in the reader's mind a system of notion placement in various zones of the brain. Throughout *Matchbooks* these notions and their mind-map placement are repeated until the reader not only comes to accept them but becomes snug and comfortable with them to the point of no longer noticing them at all. In the final chapter Lint abruptly places several of the notions in the "wrong" parts of the reader's mind-map—some readers reputedly suffered brain hemorrhages as a result (or at least, as Koryagina reports, "psychotic breaks"). It is as though the brain tries to fold over and contorts to place the notion in the "correct" position. Lint organized it so that all the necessary contortions were impossible to perform simultaneously, so that the brain literally tore.

Though Lint was running a psyche game behind the text, the story gives plenty for the reader to look at. It was satire as sacrament, as Arkwitch storms heaven in search of a cipher key. God had overlooked something—sinning honors personality. "The heaven penetration program was a tesseract looking several ways so it could recall the way out. It set down on roots like bent cigarettes, the stay short-lived."

"You didn't know god very well before coming here," said the angel impassively. Behind it, undecanted angels in rows. "You should have done more research prior to dying."

So the angel thought Arkwitch was dead.

The Phosphorus Tarot of Matchbooks is a flashbook of angelic schematics and Sacred Strategy, a sort of herringbone cypher flowing behind the text. That pattern is reproduced in the fabric of a disoriented Arkwitch's reentry—time-exits are fringed with hooks, tearing his armor away. Landing in a forgotten colony of vines and scrub, Arkwitch crawls into the lap of a gold Buddha and is blanketed in butterflies. The end of his sanity is like a sunrise.

TWENTY-THREE

EASY PROPHECY

Oppressive smithereens ○ *gently meddling with the future* ○
prophecy humor ○ *America's make-believe* ○ *"Reality is the thing*
that doesn't need to be asserted" ○ Nous sentant des ailes ○ *cramming*

Whatever happened to the prophecies that never happened?
Where do those beauties go? This was the basic premise of Lint's
most all-American books, the *Easy Prophecy* series: *Die Miami,
Doomed and Confident,* and the uncompleted *Zero Learned from
Nero.* Lint pitched the series as a high-blown concept franchise
like *Dune* and tried not to laugh. No one could contact his agent,
Robert Baines, but Doubleday waved the deal through.

The premise of the books is simplicity itself. Transported
from a free America to one very closely resembling that of the
1980s, nervy draughtsman Helio Lashpool tries to prove to everyone that he does not belong in this pseudo-USA. But as the years

pass, he comes to feel that every nation traverses different versions of itself over time, and at the end of the first book he stands gutted and dazed before blanket hypocrisy and a media made up of oppressive smithereens. In an apparent foretelling of Bush Junior's reign Lashpool remarks: "Better than a leader smart enough to lie is a leader stupid enough to genuinely believe what he's saying." There's a little bit of Kafka about Lashpool. Lint's interpretation of Kafka's *The Trial* was that the guilt felt by K— and depended upon by the state—derives from his having allowed the state to become so strong in the first place. K therefore ultimately accepts his punishment.

In the second book Lashpool is trying to send messages across the reality bands or back in time to himself. Lint wondered at the lack of humor in prediction (which he put down to the fact that humor requires precision) and at how the style of a particular prophecy changes slightly each time the date for it is set back. "I got the idea for that from *Die Miami*'s deadline. When they first told me the deadline, I assured them I wouldn't be able to meet it, yet when the deadline arrived and I told them again that, no, I couldn't meet it, they acted surprised. They weren't surprised the first time they heard the facts, but were surprised the second time."

Lashpool's messages range from the obvious, that human civilization will end ("Sapphires and salt will reunite"), to the evaded ("Most people approach the subject of suicide determined to be baffled"). He sends the messages back by emitting them in imitation of a reverse echo building up to the loud and clear message itself. At the subpatternist level the reverse echo continues into the past.

"From the midst of the future you call to your present self," Lashpool thinks, "whining of the lack of wonders." He sets about tracking down others who may be misplaced like himself, and locates Calvin Bridges, an obscure author with an oxygen fetish and a gift for making a merely old idea look classical. "Masks in collections have no blood," the old man tells Lashpool. "Night done by scientists would be a bit flat and taste of powdery lead." He shows Lashpool a clock of iron, gas in its veins. He has created a literary alkaloid that pours through counterweights and says it reproduces the present culture in that it is a system so fragile that it really may be safer to sustain the problem than to solve it. "We put history behind us so we can more convincingly exhibit surprise when it bites us in the ass. Poison be merry, you are due to inherit a world." The most-quoted line from the two published books is: "America's make-believe is more dangerous than its reality." Truth is unpopular because it doesn't have a dependent need to be liked or believed—its independence seems like unfriendliness. *Doomed* ends in a sort of showdown between two Lashpools in the Nevada flatlands.

In the unpublished *Zero Learned from Nero* a Lashpool-led revolution creates a downpour of blood into the underworld as those above finally find expression. One politician explains to the firing squad that he followed a particular policy merely because it was eleven times more interesting than common sense. Lint's notes describe Lashpool "emerging on top of dogma like a boy on top of a haystack." He isn't really convinced by the revolution—he just wants to speed up whatever history is in progress toward human extinction. "This planet won't breathe easy till weeds conquer the corridor."

One critic noted that *Doomed* was so "stupid" that he refused to explain it. Another quipped that the book was "for novelty purposes only."

In Taos, Lint was writing steadily and building a winged and sailed vimana in the yard. Failing to find a church that did not demand he repent of his imagination, Lint flirted with Bahai and finally settled into a nameless one of his own invention. "Reality is the thing that doesn't need to be asserted," he yelled at a barber the one time he visited the local hairdressers and caused such fear and concern that he never visited again, allowing his beard and hair to grow large and scary. This did not deter the increasing number of fans who showed up to hear some sort of wisdom or just bathe in a guru's mysterious securities. Some erstwhile fans seemed to be simply following the trend—Lint was stalked by a misguided groupie (Ann Coulter) who had never read his work but repeatedly demanded "lobster sex." "She went way over the top," says Chris Diana. "And she didn't really understand what it was about. It was embarrassing for the rest of us." Apparently she was convinced she was married to Lint.

Before starting in on the last installment of the *Easy Prophecys*, he got into a book he had planned throughout the eighties, the lush opus *Clowns and Locusts*. Lint seems to have been cramming, as though aware that he didn't have much time. But in his last years he stated an absolute conviction that his work would make no difference. "Like snow," said Twain, "satire lasts a while on firm ground." But Lint knew satire was less than weak and that even a convenient church was shelter from it.

TWENTY-FOUR

CLOWNS AND LOCUSTS

Soylent scream ∘ *garnet* ∘ *acceleration* ∘ UltraLint ∘
The Jarkman ∘ *'cause I'm done dead already* ∘ UFO *flap*

Lint says in *Arse* that when he suggested *Clowns and Locusts* to John Harklerod, the Doubleday editor walked away at twenty miles an hour. But it was a gift to fans, who view it not so much as a book as a gold-geared reliquary case. Others see it as the living quartz *Zohar* from his "Glove Begs for Skeleton" story.[19] At first seeming to be a sort of shirttails sequel to *Matchbooks*, it soon goes totally berserk with a toy-town intensity.

The book begins with Barry Soylent, a fella whose higher self doesn't seem to be keeping up its end of the bargain, explaining to his nervous nephew that his forehead is about to "anabolically scramble":

"My every waking moment is dedicated to perfecting this scowl. See?"

"It's ... good."

"Yes it is good. It's just about the best by now, why not?"

The old man becomes increasingly belligerent about the condition of his frown until, standing suddenly, he exerts forward strangely, forcing a blast of pure assertion from his brow. "An idea hot as a garnet sizzled out through his forehead, leaving a mystery burn like a bullet hole."

Lint says this was an account of birthing the book itself. And it seemed he'd entered an awful influence—a white-matter ride down some oblique airstrip where the landscape of notions suddenly bottomed out into stomach-lurching chasms. Gem-yellow eye blasts kicked neon through his head, trail-stains containing dense information like code brew. Green gold-leaf was rippling across the page like the liquid wisdom in a peppermint bible. Lint couldn't believe this shit was still happening to him at sixty-four. Stupendous megaverse glimpses in the corner of the room were a young man's game. He says he later found some of the sentences branded into the adobe walls as though pressed into soft wax.

"The book accelerates so suddenly it blows the eyebrows off your mind," says fan Simon Gilbert in *Parasite Regained Zine*.

After a seeming eternity sampling gem-quality pains, Soylent winds up cramping in a crusty phone booth, developing the reptilian skin of a pineapple. But in the alkaline flush of the window reflection he sees his face young against the night. Behind him is simpleton paradise, the burning sweetness of the world, an acid street. When he looks again he sees a portrait of a dried man, nervy hands over the brain as his own thinning hair slips through his fingers like a lifeline. The man-thing is found in diced green glass, the situation pulling away into miniature—the world is nothing but a black theory in space, crawling with professionals. It's a vision of relaxed, natural injustice. God fights us on his own turf—everywhere. One ever-deepening commandment saves time and ink, and this is how *Clowns and Locusts* itself operates—you can unpack it forever. Every sentence expands in all directions at once and it becomes immersive to the point of hallucination. The story falls away into a heavy fever-dream, a sort of constant metamorphosis parade. Ideas turn corners on themselves and thump axes in their own backs. It jams everything so far over that many fans refer to the book as *UltraLint*.

"And would it kill you to give it a plot?" says a note from John Harklerod at Doubleday.

Some readers would call the whirling screed a compound miracle. Some were embarrassingly enthusiastic, as when William West said: "It's so forward-thrusting it ought to be fitted with a cowcatcher!" and added "Really!"

Pat Scarlett (whose by-the-numbers best seller *Snow Falling on Hot Chocolate* made her a bundle in the mid-nineties) called it "the sort of book that sets you thinking of all the things you'd like to do if you get out alive."

Lint discovered in his last few years of life that flight from commerce was like a drug—he couldn't get enough of it. In 1991 he heard that his old story "The Jarkman," which had been optioned eight years before, would be going into production. There was no way he could believe this until he saw it on the big screen but, anyway, he found with a certain light-headedness that he didn't care about it. The movie was made, of course, starring Johnny Depp as the luckless Jarkman Jones, and it started bringing a new audience to Lint's books two weeks after he cashed out.

But when told about the production he never bothered to contact the movie people. At the time Lint was an amiable bird of prey in a potato-colored coat, his head a nova in disguise. Wandering through a generic chain store and forgetting which town he was in, Lint pondered the possibility of teleporting from one location to another by using such identical stores to convince yourself that you're already there (a spatial version of Jack Finney's mind-set time-travel technique).

Lint had begun to find that his head, though as high-res as ever, could only run six or seven parallel thought strands at a time. "It doesn't limit clarity," he told me in 1992. "But it makes comparison a longer process. I have to juggle now, because I can't see everything at once." He compensated by selecting initial subjects that were farther apart so that the subjects implied in the expanse between them (which Lint could mentally "see") would be greater. "It's like a stretch of colorful gum," he explained. "And here's the beauty part—the perilous edge of betrayal is like an electric current." Lint seemed to have located a vein and settled there.

This was also the time of a Lint doppelgänger appearing in Mexico City during a UFO "flap," dancing jerkily in the street beneath a dozen indistinct silver "spheres." The Lint in Taos denied having danced in Mexico City that year.

His chins were to treble in the coming months.

TWENTY-FIVE

IN PERSON

"Gigantic pleasure rockets" ◦ *backpackers* ◦
"Dance to feedback old man" ◦ *Silent is the city that applauds integrity* ◦
real pumped ◦ *god trying to be funny* ◦ *acolytes* ◦
The truth is never wrong ◦ *scorpion globe paperweights* ◦ *consensus*

In New Mexico corners, ghosts of the wrong opinions come to settle down. I visited Taos in 1992 in the hope of interviewing Lint, my copies of *I Blame Ferns* and *Jelly Result* having already fallen apart. It was a time when he was working on *Clowns and Locusts*, *The Man Who Gave Birth to His Arse* and, many fans believe, a great deal more besides.

In the front yard, weeds vibrate with wind and in among them lies an ornamental idiot. There are little barrel cacti and heliotrope, the only flower whose name sounds like a Victorian flying machine. The door is answered by a striking Native American girl, Lint's girlfriend Lois Quijas. She invites me in but says Lint is doing what she calls his "beard exercises." As I sit in the drawing room I hear terrifying screams from elsewhere in the house. Quijas quietly brings tea. I look around at furniture as old as God and a mantel clock made of sponge. Strange carvings. A window shows Veda sails growing in the back garden. A local newspaper had reported that the author carved some "gigantic pleasure rockets" in his yard—actually vimana replicas. Warped by several New Mexico snows, some now resembled effigies of Jeb Bush. Lint had dug in the garden to a depth of seven yards.

Turning to the front window, I was startled to see the world outside inverted, sky below and earth above—the glass pane was a slightly concave lens.

Then Lint filled the room like a buffalo, with a haircut like a Rolodex and a graying beard like a surf explosion. Skin gray as a mushroom. Old people can be scary because you can never tell how much they know. Even a moron who's never garnered a single notion from a lifetime's observations can look at you in a sagging, sad way and appear the wisest or most condemnatory sage on the planet. Consider the appalling codger in *Dragons of Aggrazar*. But just when I was ready to bolt he backed off and showed me a varnished china ornament of a red cow with a fish's face. "Maybe that'll satisfy you," he said in a deeply resonant voice. "No? You're a tough man to please." He placed it carefully back on the mantel and waved me out back, showing me the garage where he was carving a huge sculpture of a swordfish. Blond wood-curls littered the floor. He told me the dead oaf in the front yard was his work also. Then he coughed like a grave and we went to sit in a couple of iron chairs in the warm garden. He sat there until body and brain were one, then said he'd read the only story I'd had published anywhere at the time. "Your 'turbo saint' is taking his largely risk-free existence for granted."

"That's the whole point, Mr. Lint."

"It's the point is it. I thought you being smart was the point. Well I'll let it slide. Because you made an appointment." These days Lint was being accosted by disciples galore. Attentive to his legend, kids saw him as a proto-stoner, historic. "They show up under backpacks the size of an electric chair to survey the ancient glories of my talent, never guessing that aforesaid talent is still in damn near full working order. They tell me, 'Dance to feedback, old man.' A temporary lion sits just as heavy on m'chest." He talked a while about his current intensive writing schedule.

Quijas came out with juice.

"When I met Lois, I couldn't take my lights off her. She keeps me in check. Henry Heimlich—imagine being married to that guy! So you're from England? No room to move and a tax disk on your coffin. Poor kid."

"Why did you come back to New Mexico?"

"Where to go, for peace? Silent is the city that applauds integrity. Out here..." He trailed off. "A shame that the solutions to this world's problems are so lacking in glamor. There are no explosions or big noises involved. They're not visually exciting. They're difficult to cover in short clips and sound bites. They involve a different kind of revenge than the war kind—one that's quiet and takes a million years. Patience and planning don't look plucky."

"You like the countryside."

"Even my bandages are made of cowhide."

Lint had recently been hired to create a tourist slogan for the town and came up with "Holiday parasites are welcome in a way, aren't they?" They had also rejected his proposals for Bastard Awareness Week.

"People pretend life's a decision, but there's no commitment in a dawn, there's no heart of it—just the momentum of continuing. Best to tell the authorities you're deceived, though, eh? Give them something."

"Do you feel at all flattered by people's admiration for your work?"

"My own pleasure in it is primary, but of course I care. A fellow may appear hard and inflexible, but every shell holds flesh, that's what I say."

I looked up. The sky was dyed in patterns.

"But I won't be dragged under by my anchor," he said, and drank some orange. It seemed he thought one day the utter certainty of definition would pin him and allow the valuable portions of his meaning to escape—he hoped not to be alive to witness it. "Here I am at the end of my life, my cheeks amounting only to a nuisance," he smiled.

And the Fantastic Lemon experience?

"Unfortunately the absorption into cosmic consciousness is the ultimate herding instinct. It's not for me. My eternity days are over." He'd more or less decided the event was him catching the sky giving a discreet yawn. "Don't get me wrong, I'm real pumped about this dying thing. Who isn't? I intend to subject myself to the inclemencies of decomposition as if they were giving prizes."

Lint pointed to the ossuary TV that a fan had given him. "They're not real bones," he said. "But it's amazing, isn't it?" It was the only TV he had and it didn't receive conventional signals. Lint talked in detail about the ossuary church in Kutna Hora.

Did he have any funeral plans?

"Well, death's moved on by the time we start making a fuss of it. No sense in a big send-off." He looked at the garden awhile. "Dying is a sacrament, and an inconvenience."

"So what's pain?"

"Pain is God trying to be funny. That's how out-of-touch It is."

Everything was broken up as three fans arrived—two girls and a boy. I saw the prolonged collapse of Lint's brow surpassing disapproval into some parched lunar realm of blasted condemnation. He stood and went inside, but seemed to undergo some transformation into civility once actually in the company of these fans. The afternoon was spent with the kids, whom he referred to as "praxis bandits," asking questions about Arkwitch, the Caterer, and other characters while giggling like tarts. The boy told me in confidence that he'd heard there was some weird contraption in the basement, like the arcane vehicle in Pal's movie of *The Time Machine*. One of the girls asked Lint if he would write a fourth Arkwitch book, and he replied that there was a "halloween likelihood" of his writing another. "You can scrap that idea." The other girl assured me that the old man didn't mean it and was merely "flirting with McCoy."

I had heard tales from other visitors. Some kids had asked him to demonstrate "shallow vanishing" from *Jelly Result*, at which he told them to demonstrate "deep vanishing" and get the hell out. One acolyte, Cheryl Daly, has claimed to have seen Lint perform the former etheric maneuver: "He went, ostensibly to get something out of the fridge, stopped and turned back a little as if to make sure none of us was looking, then stepped in a weird way, sort of carving diagonally out of existence. He was gone for an hour. He was nowhere in the house. Then he walked downstairs and everything carried on. He looked well rested" (from Daly's *Brainfucker*).

I never saw Lint doing such a trick. Searching for the toilet, I ended up going down some steps and turned on a string light. I was in a basement workshop full of woodwork and gadgets, and on one table was a large transparent book, probably made of Perspex or heavy molded plastic, lit from below like a *Day the Earth Stood Still* special effect. It was inscribed in purple with warnings and hopes:

"The future's fucked. There are too many masks in the egg."

"A recurring dream is a revelation on redial."

"All atoms have equal value."

"The truth is never wrong."

I heard some clattering above and got out fairly swiftly, though I wasn't particularly scared.

Upstairs, Lint was still entertaining. "You can oppose in slumber," he was saying. "Not many people realize it. And learn to enjoy those dreams in which you find yourself naked in public— they can, if you let them, be a right laugh and stop the other people in the dream from acting so boring."

"Sleep is a waste of life," said the boy.

After a pause Lint gave the opinion the ceremonial snort it demanded.

Late afternoon I had to leave—heading toward Albuquerque where I would view the site of the old Consolation Playhouse. Lint, now sounding tired and boxed in tedium, said, "If consensus drips in your eyes like a snowman, consider that it might be yours."

I looked back—he was at the door. His ears were red as strawberries. He seemed to be waiting for the worst.

TWENTY-SIX

LINT IS DEAD II—
RUMORS, CLUES, AND LOST WORKS

Stoked ∘ *preferably in velvet* ∘ *liars invade verdant Eden* ∘
sightings ∘ Jellypressure ∘ *the subtle game* ∘ *cults and fan clubs* ∘
the future as a statue in a fountain ∘ *Lint's dreamers*

On July 13, 1994, Lint had a near-death experience, followed immediately by death. The cause was a massive brain hemorrhage that seemed to replicate the garnet-sizzle birthing of a book described in *Clowns and Locusts*. Those around Lint confirm that he had been stoked for his death, though he had not visited a doctor and had no external confirmation that anything was wrong with him. A small funeral service occurred three days later, Rouch reading from the *Matchbooks* passage in which Lint describes heaven as a shambles and God as "unkempt," while nature disassembles his old body: "biological traffic expanding through me, tributary life like a root system teasing me apart."

The starchy Rouch read the piece with quite a bit of gusto and raised some smiles among friends. "No sense preaching against personal circumstance. Bullying the funeral procession won't get them dancing."

The long coffin was lowered. Rouch takes up the story: "I went back to pay my respects at the house and a massive garden sculpture of Jeb Bush fell over sideways, smashing almost every bone in my body. It rather colored the rest of my visit."

Still smarting from Lint's first demise, the media waited awhile until assured that he was truly dead and that no personal consequence would proceed from praise. When the floodgates of laudation were officially opened, this and the *Jarkman* movie raised Lint's profile far higher than it had ever been. Though some see it as a tragedy that he died before setting out upon the uncharted waters of success, Lint himself defined success as "being able to do whatever the hell I want, preferably in velvet." *The Jarkman* hardly fits this description. Depp's appointment as a sheriff of the old West, with only a hedgehog for a friend, distant from moments actually lived, his duels a sort of hypnotic combat, and his final shot a long-coat stance against the movie's souped-up sky, is a modern spaghetti Western punctuated by the occasional gnomic pronouncement, the classic being "To be out of step is to be free."

Certain areas of the press still seemed uncertain as to how to pitch the late author. PLAYWRITE SHUNNED LIONS went the headline to the London *Times* obituary. The *Washington Post* used the headline AUTHOR CORRODED BY STEAM and called him an "ambiloquent neckverser," whatever that is. Other obituaries bemoaned the wisdom of hindsight, wailing about readers' vulnerability to

Lint and how, in an industry designed to screen out originality, Lint had fallen through the cracks in the system.

Lois Quijas refused to speak to the press about Lint and has maintained this policy to the present day. This has been used by certain fans to shore up the "faked death" conspiracy case. It is known that Lint had considered being buried under the pen name Isaac Asimov. The death was sudden and unexpected to readers at large, and Quijas was viewed with Yoko-like suspicion by those who didn't know her. The "hidden message" crowd brought back trophies such as this line in *Fanatique*: "Love is: never taking it seriously as liars invade verdant Eden" (the first letters of each word spelling the message "Lint is alive"). It all combined to create a bunch of Hendrixal scenarios in which Lint dyed his beard and was transported to a village in Spain.[20]

Hundreds of Lint sightings are made every year, though these are usually found to be sightings of a store Santa Claus. William West has written of having had contact with a person claiming to be Jeff Lint in 1998. This tale, involving secret meetings in a Washington parking garage and so on, is compelling bullshit. West states that Lint occasionally works as a store Santa Claus, but this seems too much of a comedown for the man who was once Woolworth's unofficial "Monstrous Poet." Critic Leo Brady believed the theory, however, and supposedly went up to a Santa and sneered "Kecksburg looks pretty good right now, doesn't it?" The jolly man punched Brady to the ground and began kicking him brutally, even breaking away from store security later on to start in on the dazed, bowed critic again. Some commentators have presented the response as proof that this was indeed Lint. Brady's nose was displaced so precisely that nature tried to rectify the anomaly by growing another one beside it. This freakery was as nothing compared to the dessicated horror found in Robert Baines's office when police finally forced an entry in 1996. The empty eye sockets of Lint's agent had gazed wistfully out upon Manhattan for forty years.

At Lint's death, word was already out about the autobiographical *Arse* fragment and the uncompleted *Zero Learned from Nero*. But the speculation as to "lost" and unpublished works has spun out of control. There are rumors of a dime Western, *He Died With His Fins On*, and a noir detective novel *Buck Twenty* (the purported text of which has lately circulated on the Net), a strange book called *Pumpkin*, a sequel to *Jelly Result* to be called *Jellypressure*, and a videogame, *Red Death Taxi*, in which a crazy plague-ridden cabdriver must career through New York infecting as many passengers as possible. Several movie scripts are said to be floating around, including something called *Alba's Wolves*. Lint scholars have also rampaged through *Astounding*, certain that one of Lint's stories hides there. Juvenilia is also up for grabs—the original manuscript of Lint's first-ever story, "Mister Flabbycheeks Shouts Trash," sold at auction for $300 (£9).

There is also the matter of the Corediss program that extends Lint's theory of nanodissing, the inscription of insults at the molecular level. During Lint's lifetime it was thought that this was mere postmodern art, that it wouldn't be felt by anyone without an explanation by the artist, and probably not even then. But it was found that certain molecular reconfigurations accorded with certain physical manifestations. In fact, certain brands or families of insult coincided with certain reactions. Lint supposedly intensified his work (at the theoretical, computer-model level) to the

Tachyon Insult and Graviton Barracking, and, via string theory, worked toward the Unified Insult. Of the various works claimed for Lint since his death, this seems one of the most characteristic, allied as it is to Lint wedge theory and other forms of tagging.

The late nineties saw the start of an industry of Lint apocrypha, some embarrassing imitations purporting to be Lint and wasting everyone's time, and a few competent homages (the best being Enkhornish's *Jeff Lint Is Boiling Forever in Hell, Alas*). But the trend worries the more serious Lint scholars—as Lint himself said, "Substitute something down the centuries and it becomes the real thing as far as those bastards are concerned."

Fans' beloved theory of faked death and covert works would seem to imply that rather than spending a life rampaging through the English language like a buffalo, Lint was in fact playing a deep and subtle game. But conspiracy is not required to support this. Lint always had an agenda that split diagonally across the standard grooves—in fact he seems to have been unaware that such grooves existed. Lucking onto the circumstance of being seen by most as faded and unsuitable, his later years concealed a neglected and fertile talent cellar hopping with frogs. The urge to add to his oeuvre through fakery seems like the cheapest kind of book-celeb hysteria. "But then," says Alan Rouch, "Jeff would expect people to miss the point."

For example, there exists a so-called Guild of Perfect Interruption (Hyperquills) who use *The Stupid Conversation* as their Bible. Internal power-plays in the fan club Hyperquill Enterprises resulted in the expulsion of those participants with a sense of proportion and the former pranksters quickly became cod-occult. The Guild has lately established a sort of "high ritual"

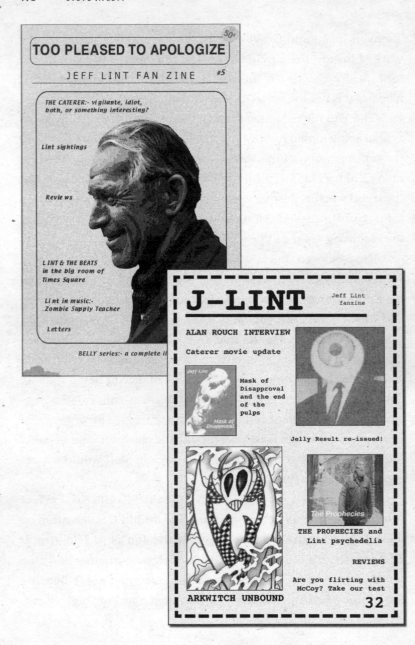

TOO PLEASED TO APOLOGIZE   50¢

JEFF LINT FAN ZINE   #5

THE CATERER:- vigilante, idiot, both, or something interesting?

Lint sightings

Reviews

LINT & THE BEATS in the big room of Times Square

Lint in music:- Zombie Supply Teacher

Letters

BELLY series:- a complete li

J-LINT   Jeff Lint fanzine

ALAN ROUCH INTERVIEW

Caterer movie update

Mask of Disapproval and the end of the pulps

Jeff Lint
Mask of Disapproval

Jelly Result re-issued!

THE PROPHECIES and Lint psychedelia

REVIEWS

Are you flirting with McCoy? Take our test

ARKWITCH UNBOUND

32

Lint mass, including air-kerning and Huskanoy photos, and a liturgical call and reply of "What have the walking dead?" / "A brain stem like a tow bar." A strange side-product of this has been the production of the Arkwitchboard, a Ouija board that gives a choice of answers ranging from "Realize I am laughing" to "I won't prevent it" and "Concealed by the background."

Since 1997 the Jeff Lint Fan Club has held festivals as a remedy to the lunatic fringe and to the humorless scholars who appointed themselves to pick over the disputed fortune of Lint's genius. The first conference was held at the Red Lion Inn in Portland, Oregon, historic venue for the September 1989 meeting at which U.S. military officials instructed Iraqi technicians in how to detonate a nuclear bomb. But the Lint conference didn't benefit from the funding of Honeywell and Hewlett-Packard—it was a shoestring affair characterized by malfunctioning projections of *Catty* and nervous anoraks standing to speak about Arkwitch and faked detritus. Contraband copies of Lint's *Star Trek* script changed hands for large sums. The meetings have gone from strength to strength, with Alan Rouch attending twice and a certain Professor Dystrak reading from Robert Baines's coroner's report as gruesome evidence slides flashed up behind him. Rounds of *Platypus Payback* were played one year, resulting in a massive cleaning bill from the hotel. In 2002 Elsa Carnesky appeared, having only recently realized the selfish/shellfish misunderstanding.

Many commentators are harmless and touching. There is a subcult similar to the *Catty* dreamers, in which uberfans describe dreams where Lint crops up. He appears variously as a knowing, enigmatic and powerfully comforting presence who gives a wink and explodes away in purple light; as a ghost in agony, its skull rattling like a dried gourd; as a pratfalling angel with Victorian frame wings; as a poolside millionaire; as an inconstant, guttering image which tries desperately to dictate the opening paragraphs of a new novel; as Felix Arkwitch in the lap of the Buddha.

Gore Vidal has described Lint as entering the world of letters like a fat man jumping into a swimming pool. The ripples are spreading to this day, and those splashed by the initial impact are still standing drenched like comedy straight men.

TWENTY-SEVEN

THE MAN WHO GAVE BIRTH TO HIS ARSE

*Saddled ∘ scrubbing tombstones ∘ don't thank the shark ∘
the claymore principle of creation ∘ savoring regret ∘ The Vermilion Equation
∘ intravenous cheats ∘ for I am the way ∘ new colors*

In Jeff Quiros Engram's obituary of Lint, "Dead, eh? How's That
Workin' Out For Ya?" he portrayed a writing career that consisted
of "a blowtorch and one man's dreams." In Lint's own unfinished
autobiography, *The Man Who Gave Birth to His Arse*, Lint recalls
deciding early that he'd prefer life to come out and fight rather
than dropping a thousand bad-luck hints a day. "I was saddled
with this nonsense on July 6, 1928, and the minute I arrived I
knew events were not going to suit me. And the advent of my ability to twitch my arms and legs a bit caused me no great consolation." School was a training ground for indifference. Lint recalls
that as a child he thought the word *imbecile* meant some kind of
beacon for traffic. "The easy wisdom of youth," he writes. "As one
who will of necessity learn the art of conversation from his ene-
mies, an honest man must be careful to note when a word does not
yet exist to express a situation. I thought 'I'll invent a theme of my
own, something about the language of future scars.'"

He cut a frayed figure in the world, a man who voluntarily
spoke the truth on countless occasions, who lived for love of

unnamed colors and the glee of releasing vertical bombs of resentment. "The problem of seeing clearly is that you find yourself surrounded on all sides by liars," Lint wrote, "and stand the chance of going completely insane." He would often suffer "firmament vertigo" when gazing up at the stars. In response to astronomers' observations that the universe seemed to be rushing away from us, he remarked, "Wouldn't you?"

Lint knew that words are counterfeit symbols: "A word is a photo of gold," he said. Satire was like scrubbing tombstones with a toothbrush, but honorable nevertheless. "Of course the inhabitants of this world complain in vain, but this is no reason to cease stating the truth. It seems to me we shouldn't thank the shark and count our blessings. Nor wait for a savior, an accident, or an alien the color of a Band-Aid." His very awareness of words' limitations made him run around like some nutter with a blowpipe, creating a career described variously as a triumph, a benchmark for defeat, a systemized kitsch torus, hell on a stick, a ferocious bluff, the revenge of the Alexandrian library, a strange honking sound, not too shabby, glyph contraband, nutty slack, exhausting, a catalog of fevers, and "gear."

Far from basking in disapproval, Lint was usually unaware that he was being disapproved of. "Pause sheet lightning and scrawl on that," the young Lint advised himself while indulging in highwire affrontery and cipher psychosis. "I'll tear my words and body till they bleed into each other." He considered a career conducted at a velocity that, even if he blew apart, meant the end of the enterprise would be of adequate interest. But this claymore principal of creation is belied by his long quiet work on the Arkwitch trilogy. In regard to bad reviews, he said "Hopefully such expressions of disapproval are stages in the journey toward being cut loose entirely."

There are chapters of historical interest in *Arse*, such as the one on his JFK experience, "The Trauma That Passed Me By," and his summary of theories regarding the Fantastic Lemon: "Luminescence to one side, luminescence to the other—you ask why I was on the verge?"

Lint described sleep, writing, and sex as his greatest joys in life and expressed bitterness that the last so often fell victim to some larger and less interesting scheme of the Almighty.

"Does the chance exist after the failure to take it? The missed opportunity like a mineral fish preserved in cliffs?" Lint savored regret like a fine wine. "It does in fact serve as a sort of file reference system," he said, "or mental diary, as it gives me at least one thing to remember with clarity from every day of my life." But Lint is not maudlin in *Arse* and expresses the wish to be caught in some kind of golden Vedic crossfire until "refined to a knob of russet gore." To some observers it seemed Lint had hastened the death schedule. Lint described the transition as like stone steps going down into water. He imagined his debut underground: "My first day in the reverse-nursery of the grave!"

At his death Lint was working on something called the Vermilion Equation, by which almost bottomless amounts of retrievable information could be sunk into minute bits of text. The equation seems to hinge on the notion that nothing is so strange that it can't be true. Adjunct to his calculations were mandala-like schematics resembling the paintings of Paul Laffoley. One is labeled "The Alontvashid. This particular page. In the shuffle of eternity even this was once perhaps the flushed center of something."

Lint compared the Internet to pulps such as *Weird Tales*—
that magazine was now all but lost to decay, releasing the scent of
cinnamon and sandalwood, and he wondered what would become
of thoughts, correspondence and stories dependent upon contin-
ual support and electric current. He factored this into his legacy
when, referring to Shelley's *Ozymandias* and seeming to forebode
events after his death, he remarked that he had always found it
overly optimistic to expect the two towers to remain standing.
Would he be remembered as a treasure trove of heaven access-
cheats and intravenous smarts or, as he suspected, left out of the
history of literature for screwing up the continuity? There were
those who set about paving this literary sugar field immediately. "I
saw a book by Lint once," said Frederick Weisberg, "but it was
called *Nose Furnace*, and there was no question of my reading it."

"He was like an hour of Technicolor film showing up in 1900
then going missing forever," says Simon Gilbert. "An urban myth.
And who can be a legend more than once?"

Fellow synesthetes understood Lint when he said he'd seen a
new color at the point where green turns into orange, and that it
felt like the vinegar-flavored singing itch he got in his arm marrow
sometimes. There were reversed acidic blue golds, green golds,
and purple golds that show up in music and certain suburban
garage doors at twilight. There were chemicals essential for the
operation of time, words redefined to permit atrocity, atrophy
speeded up and termed employment, unrecorded love under
asphalt, slavery too close for the eye's focus, whole lives impaled
on society like carousel horses, and the hook throne of approval.

To those who value these truths, Lint remains the child who
tried to unearth the bruises underground.

LINT QUOTATIONS

"Civilization is the agreement to have gaps between wars."
Prepare to Learn

"Of course the government wants us to kick heroin. And they're
not asking us to do anything they haven't done themselves."
Die Miami

"Television is light filled with someone else's anxiety."
Zero Learned from Nero

"An optimist has nothing but miracles to rely on."
Slogan Love

"Has murder ever been patented? There's a cash cow."
Prepare to Learn

"Modern architecture is about endurance on all sides."
I Blame Ferns

"Waxen saviors hang on the dash and I buy a hot dog.
Such are the inequalities of charisma."
"The Harrowing Squid"

"Pain is God trying to be funny. That's how out-of-touch It is."
Interview, 1992

"I seem to be outliving my ears."
Kiss Me, Mr. Patton (screenplay)

"Cold wind and candidates—that's Washington to a tourist."
"An Ominous Mirth"

"Water is Italian—it persists by adapting to everything,
then slipping away."
Prepare to Learn

"When the abyss gazes into you, bill it."
Interview, 1979

"All cities are designed for the same scenarios."
The Man Who Gave Birth to His Arse

"A shame that the solutions to this world's problems are so
lacking in glamor. There are no explosions or big noises
involved. . . . Patience and planning don't look plucky."
Interview, 1992

"*War*—the meaning of the term has diversified to exploit more
markets. You'll notice the same hasn't happened for terrorism."
Doomed and Confident

"Drugs suffer so."
Die Miami

"No one is blander than a jeweler, have you noticed?"
Turn Me into a Parrot

"Employment is atrophy speeded up."
The Stupid Conversation

"Your wife is positively radiant with repression."
Frightful Murder at Hampton Place (screenplay)

"You Must Be This Gullible To Vote."
Die Miami

"Gods will be dragged screaming from the ether."
The Caterer

"Every ten seconds somewhere in the world,
someone is realizing I'm right."
Interview, 1970

"Debt circulates, the most emphatic form of communication."
"Cats Receive Broadcasts"

"I never met a challenge I didn't."
"Epidermal Dawns"

"Lying is the new black."
Doomed and Confident

"Most people approach the subject of suicide
determined to be baffled."
Doomed and Confident

"The devil is God found out."
"Dove in Head"

"Exile is relief disguised as penance."
I Blame Ferns

FOOTNOTES

1. Rouch has suggested that this was the origin of Lint's wearing women's clothes when submitting work to publishers. Campbell supposedly said "Pop it through the mail, you know our address" and Lint thought he said "Poppet, for a male you know how to dress" and somehow got the notion that presentation was crucial. Most Lint scholars reject the theory.
2. The three books are *One Less Bastard*, *Nose Furnace*, and the story collection *I Eat Fog*. It may appear that Lint delivered books 2 and 3 at a leisurely pace, but he seems to have made a genuine attempt to give *Jelly Result* to Rodence, finding the Never Never offices starkly empty but for a litter of unbound pages and unpaid bills. By the time Rodence surfaced again, trading as Furtive Labors Books, *Jelly Result* was part of a deal with Doubleday.
3. PULP WRITER'S PUMP-ACTION HEAD CLAIM probably originates from several people's description of Lint as resembling a duck, with accompanying

impersonations. SF AUTHOR IN "CHARMED WONDERBOY" OUTBURST derives from his appearance at the LA Sci-Fi Convention during which he had some sort of seizure and told the crowd a totally different version of *Jelly Result,* topping it with the pronouncement that he was "alarmed and overjoyed" to be there. WRITER IS MADE OF CHIMP MEAT seems linked to his mention of evolutionary theory while visiting New England.

4. The resulting stories included "Chest-deep in My Own Jelly," "My Jelly Is Fantastic," "The Jelly Cannot Lie," "Woe Unto My Jelly," "Jelly Invasion," "My Jelly Is an Eye," "My Eye Is a Jelly," "Fearing My Jelly," "I Married a Jelly," "Look Out—Jellies," "A Punch to the Jelly," "Rest Your Beer on My Jelly," "Jellying Out," "A Jellyful of Murder."

5. It is not known why Lint didn't give *Ferns* to Doubleday, but his lack of input probably contributed to that company's conviction that he was dead in the mid-sixties.

6. "Hanna Barbera'll have our balls for a bolus," Arnie Waldheim is said to have shouted in the narrow corridor outside Lint's office.

7. *Blast of Merit* became the title of a Lint fanzine published in Austin, Texas, in the mid-eighties.

8. Lord Caul Pin has claimed that he was unaware of this sentiment when constructing the massive—and massively poisonous—"Earth Sandwich."

9. Among Lint fans the term "flirting with McCoy" is used in regard to someone who is not taking the situation entirely seriously.

10. In reality a delegation of political leaders had proposed to Ingersoll that he would receive the governorship nomination provided he concealed his opinions, to which he replied, "A good man should not agree to keep silent just for the sake of an office. A man owes his best thoughts to his country," and "Good-bye, gentlemen."

11. It was later proved that Ferrie trained Oswald in the Civil Air Patrol.

12. Lint's "clown in the trunk" theory falls down here, as Garrison was too large a man to fit into the trunk of a Plymouth coupe.

13. NormanMailer-earcrack.mpg.

14. See the Zombie Supply Teacher track "Diamondhead Driver" on the *Eye in the Belly* album, and of course the band Crystal City Martyrs.

15. According to an early Lint fanzine (*Belly Hazard*), the *Omen*-like *Sadly Disappointed* was actually the work of Alan Rouch, Lint writing Rouch's well-received *I Am a Centrifuge* in exchange. Rouch is silent on the matter, but *Centrifuge* does bear many of Lint's characteristic flourishes, such

as the assertion that "if you freeze gruel you have a sculpture of J. Edgar Hoover's face."

16. Some commentators have suggested that this was the terrified shrieking of the Smile Group themselves.

17. After adjustments the toy was released as Hungry Hungry Hippos.

18. Some fans have made a connection between the *Arkwitch* movie and *Buckaroo Banzai*, but the latter is actually far more inventive.

19. I disagree.

20. The coffin supposedly contains a "dirty bomb."

BIBLIOGRAPHY

Algren, Nelson. *Nonconformity*. Seven Stories Press, 1996.

"Asimov, Isaac." *Sadly Disappointed*. Pyramid Publications, 1974.

Aylett, Steve. *Shamanspace*. Codex, 2001.

Baldensperger, Philip J. *My Vagrant Vipers*. Boy's Own Paper, 1912.

Berrigan, Ted. *Bean Spasms*. Kulchur Press, 1967.

Carothers, Tom. *This Bee Is a Credit Card: The Madness of Postmodernism*. Cutter, 1990.

Celcis, Joe. *What the Devil Is This Thing? Pin Undercover in the Soviet Union*. Rove, 1988.

Central Intelligence Agency. *KUBARK Counterintelligence Interrogation Manual*.

———. *A Study of Assassination*.

———. *CIA and Guatemala Assassination Proposals, 1952-1954*.

Daly, Cheryl. *Brainfucker*. Arbor House, 1996.

Dewar, Jim. *Quantum Strumpet*. Ace, 1957.

Dewhurst, Hugh "Banzer." *My Understanding*. American Skeleton, 1975.

Eezie, Jetkid. *Broken Bones for No Good Reason*. Element, 1979.

Enkhornish, Kimmel H. *Jeff Lint Is Boiling Forever in Hell, Alas*. Vintage, 2000.

Esswell, Stan. *The Prophecies*. LP featuring Jeff Lint. Clownshow Records, 1991.

Estimate of the Situation in the Pacific and Recommendations for Action by the United States. Memo October 7, 1940, from Lieutenant Commander Arthur McCollum of the Office of Naval Intelligence to Navy Captains Walter Anderson and Dudley Knox.

Fall, The. *The Unutterable*. CD. Eagle Records, 2000.

Foote, G. W. *Was Jesus Insane?* Progressive, 1891.

Galen, Regina. *Frail Maze: The Limits of Labeling*. Rider, 1985.

Gilbert, Simon. *The Pocket Lint*. Self-published chapbook, 1991.

Gordon, Stan. *Kecksburg: The Untold Story*. Video documentary. 2001.

Gramajo, Hector. *Silent Sarcasm*. Lineland, 1982.

Herzog, Cameo. *Bailiff! Collected Adventures of the Bailiff*. Balkan, 1972.

———. *Dust We Shall Become: Collected Reviews of Cameo Herzog*. Balkan, 1969.

———. *The Empty Trumpet Quartet (Look Upon the Trumpet; Not That Trumpet; The Trumpet Is Empty; Yes, Empty)*. Gollancz, 2001.

———. *Eye On Sleeve: More Journalism of Cameo Herzog*. Balkan, 1970.

———. *The Final Seizure: More Adventures of the Bailiff*. Balkan, 1973.

———. *I Will Make You an Example*. University of California, Berkeley, 1964.

Hinton, C. H. *Scientific Romances*. Swan Sonnenschein & Co, 1886.

Hurk, Marshall. *Machine Shop Coins*. Dell Books, 1966.

———. *Snaggle Chops Deploys His Feelers*. Northwest Fantasy Book Club, 1988.

———. *Snaggle Chops Is Ambushed by His Own Jowls*. TOR, 2002.

———. *Snaggle Chops Rears Forward*. Self-published, 1994.

Ingersoll, Robert Green. *Best of Robert Ingersoll: Selections from His Writings and Speeches*. Prometheus Books, 1983.

Kafka, Franz. *The Trial*. Verlag Die Schmiede, 1925.

Lint, Jeff. *The Caterer*. Pearl Comics, 1975.

———. *Cheerful When Blamed*. Rich & Cowan, 1957.

———. *Clowns and Locusts*. Doubleday, 1994.

———. *Die Miami*. Doubleday, 1990.

——. *Doomed and Confident*. Doubleday, 1991.

——. *Dragons of Aggrazar*. Doubleday, 1970.

——. *Every Word at Once: Collected Plays of Jeff Lint*. William Hobart Press, 1985.

——. *Fanatique*. Doubleday, 1979.

——. *I Blame Ferns*. Olympia Press, 1959.

——. *I Eat Fog*. Furtive Labors, 1962.

——. *Jelly Result*. Doubleday, 1955.

——. *Lint: a Collection*. Phair Inc, 1973.

——. *The Man Who Gave Birth to His Arse*. Unpublished.

——. *Mask of Disapproval*. Rich & Cowan, 1961.

——. *Nose Furnace*. Furtive Labors, 1958.

——. *One Less Bastard*. Never Never, 1946.

——. *The Phosphorus Tarot of Matchbooks*. Doubleday, 1988.

——. *Prepare to Learn*. Lancer Books, 1966.

——. *Rigor Mortis*. Fairleigh University Press, 1973.

——. *Slogan Love*. Ace, 1957.

——. *The Stupid Conversation*. Doubleday, 1974.

——. *Turn Me into a Parrot*. Doubleday, 1962.

——. *Zero Learned from Nero*. Unpublished.

Lint, Jeff, Alan Rouch, Marshall Hurk, et al. *The Belly of the Belly: Belly Stories and Apocrypha*. Leffa, 1981.

Lord Pin. CD. Scar Garden Media, 2004.

Lowman, Robin (ed.). *"Can't You Tell? It's Everything": Essays on Catty and the Major*. Penn State University, 1999.

Mason, Tol. *Hoover's Foggy Hen*. Northcoast, 1996.

Matheson, Richard. *I Am Legend*. Nelson-Doubleday, 1954.

McIntosh, Burr. *The Little I Saw of Cuba*. F. T. Neely, 1899.

McNickle, Colin. *The Unstoppable Lord Pin*. Hod House, 1998.

Menard, Pierre. *Looting of Heaven*. La Scortia, 1923.

Moorcock, Michael. *Death Is No Obstacle*. Savoy, 1992.

Nashe, Thomas. *The Unfortunate Traveler*. C. Burby, 1594.

Nectargirl Climbs On. *Amateur Saints Blunder Through Visions and Fear of Injury*. LP. Lozada Records, 1990.

Nose Furnace. Graphic novel. Wallent Comics, 1986.

O'Connor, Sandra Day. *Stop Repeating Your Confession*. Hiibel Books, 1977.

Paine, Thomas. *Common Sense*. (Pamphlet), 1776.

Pin, Lord Caul. *The Most Handsome Man in the World*. Harvest Sweep Books, 1999.

Prince, Bob. *A Publicist at My Grave*. Myat, 2001.

Rensin, Don. *Crooked Smile*. Schirmer, 1979.

Rodence, Dean. *Disappointing Bargains: A Life*. Gotland, 1970.

Rouch, Alan. *I Am a Centrifuge*. Random, 1974.

———. *Meek Am I?* Phet-Schmidt-Umbach, 1996.

Scheuer, Michael. *JFK: A Hop, a Skip and a Jump to Judgment*. Borst, 1969.

Schultz, George. *"Check Out the Fangs": Final Words in the Bayou*. Cavitation Press, 1983.

Senser, Kate. *Holy Flame of Surprise*. Binah Press, 1993.

Shelley, P. B. *Shelley's Poems*. J. M. Dent & Sons, 1907.

Sienkel, Brandon. *A Life in Comics*. Hyperthick, 1999.

Smith, M. E. *The Post-Nearly Man*. CD. Artful Records, 1998.

Snowcroft, Brent. *Lord Pin: Danger Man*. Highranger, 1983.

Twain, Mark. *The War Prayer*. Harper Colophon, 1970.

Unofficial Smile Group, The. *The Energy Draining Church Bazaar*. LP featuring Jeff Lint. Elektra, 1969.

VanWoerkom, Jack A. *Resignation Space*. Gollancz, 2000.

Walsh, Allen (ed.). *Giant Feather*. (Stories from specialist pulp *Giant Feather*, including Lint's "Rise of the Swans.") Chaffee, 1976.

Wheeler, John. *Unfurled and Unrecognized—the Freedom of Enlightenment*. Open Court, 1929.

Witt, Peter N., and Jerome S. Rover (eds). *Spider Communication*. Princeton University Press, 1982.

Wolfowitz, Suharto. *JFK: Judgment in Two Shakes of a Lamb's Tail*. Keynes, 1977.

Yoshioka, Toshi. *The Wedger Bible*. Humboldt, 1998.

Zoffer, Beria. *JFK: Before You Can Say Jack Robinson—Judgment!* Beksinski Books, 1978.

INDEX

LIST OF ILLUSTRATIONS

ACKNOWLEDGMENTS

Special thanks to Lois Quijas for access to unfinished materials regarding *Zero Learned from Nero* and *The Man Who Gave Birth to His Arse*.

My thanks also go to the New York Police Department, the New York City Coroners' Department, the New York Guild of Pathologists, and the American Society of Literary Agents for records and analysis regarding Robert Baines.